Bill

Minor Chords and Moody Weather

Enjoy. Thanks for Reading

FRANK FLYNN

Frank Flynn

Copyright © 2023 Frank Flynn

All rights reserved. This book or any portion thereof may not be reproduced or used in any manner whatsoever without the express written permission of the publisher except for the use of brief quotations in a book review.

Chapter 1

The gentle light of dawn tumbled through the cabin window beside Eddie's bed. A breeze of remnant night air drifted through the screen. Eddie roused himself from blinking newborn to shuffling toddler. Stepping out the cabin door into the clearing, he breathed a deep breath of summer. After lighting a small fire in his burn pit, he placed a pot of water retrieved from the lake on a makeshift grill. At the edge of the clearing, he smoked a cigarette and slowly relieved himself as he waited for the water to boil. Half the boiled water was poured over a clutter of dishes in a rubber tub resting on the doorstep, the remainder kept for hot coffee.

    Early August mornings were a welcome change from the punishing heat of July. Quite perfect, really. Eddie fixed himself a cup of coffee, retrieved his pack of du Mauriers and ambled down the short, grassy slope to the lake. From his decaying dock, naked as the day he was born, Eddie surveyed the morning sun as it rose over the pink granite cliffs on the east side of the lake. It was cool but not unusually so. It wouldn't be more than fifteen minutes before beads of sweat would be coursing down his leathery, grey-tufted chest. Many years it was halfway through October before he abandoned his naked morning ritual. Sun was taken, coffee sipped, cigarettes smoked, thoughts thought.

The cabin was down a county road, off a remote, dirt side road, then nearly an hour hike north through a forest trail. The end of the trail ran a hundred metres down a hill from a high granite outcropping through a stand of sumacs and opened onto a small clearing amidst impenetrable brush and trees. The cabin was an old ski lodge trucked into the bush in pieces, then reassembled. No running water, no toilet. It sat ten metres from the lakeshore at the bottom of the hill, in the south corner of the clearing. The lake was east. The entry door was on the north side of the building, with another entry through a screened-in porch facing the lake. A thick-beamed, square box structure with a tiny bedroom, a kitchen shelf and table, an overhead storage loft, a small but effective wood stove, and a recliner of disproportionate elegance. Primitive or not, Eddie took great pride in his Algonquin refuge. And why wouldn't he? It was a wilderness paradise. Edward R. Novak was as far afield as civil men got.

Eddie often thought how easy it would be to pick up an electric water pump and run a line ten metres to the lake. But then there was the problem of electricity. He'd rigged up a few little solar panels, the combined power of which was only enough to run a handful of lights and the old bar fridge from his former office. He could add a panel to power a water pump, but even still, what would he do with the grey water? A septic system was out of the question. It didn't matter. The cabin was just fine without running water.

Seventy-seven years he'd been coming here—much of it spent in a tent—retreating to this place at every twist and corner of his life. From infancy and childhood to golden years, and all points in between. This was and had always been his sanctuary.

Eddie had never known life without it, and he'd go to his grave here if he could.

His father had acquired the land shortly after the war, and they'd come as a family. His father, Pietr; his mother, Danica; and sister, Annabel. His mother passed very young. His father, four years later. Annabel landed some unsuspecting American GI she'd met at a dance on a trip to East Hampton and moved there to be with him. She never returned to Canada and certainly never to the far-flung Almaguin Highlands of mid-Northern Ontario. In fact, Eddie heard very little from Annabel. That suited him fine.

Sun crested the cliffs across the lake. A great blue heron filched a frog from the water as Eddie lay on the rotting dock he'd spent a lifetime fishing from. He came to know the bird by watching her patterns. She perched atop a deadfall log lying amidst the shore grass twenty metres up the shoreline. Spreading the enormity of her wings, she took flight, passing a few feet above Eddie en route to the rock in the bay on the other side of his rickety dock. She paid Eddie no mind at all. He liked it that way. This was their routine.

Eddie lay naked on his back, unbothered by the ants and beetles devouring the dock boards around him. Today the notes of a Beethoven sonata played in his head and descended on him like spring rain. Edward R. Novak heard every note as clear as day. A waking extension of morning dreams. The music in Eddie's head played no less real than the many nights he'd spent at the symphony. Heat rising with the sun, adagio piano in his head, Eddie looked into the empty sky. He gave himself twenty minutes lying on his back before languidly rolling onto his belly to sun his buttocks. Twenty minutes a side. It seemed to him a perfect amount of time for warming his body, darkening his skin, creating vitamin D. Apart from these things, Eddie enjoyed the vaguely arousing sensation of heat on his skin. He'd take whatever arousal he could. It had been a long stretch since he'd known the intimacy of a woman. Longer, in fact, than he'd ever gone.

The sun climbed higher, and he knew it was time. Pushing his body off the dock, onto his knees, then to his feet, Eddie walked to the end of the dock and stood no more than a few seconds before plunging into the lake. The sweat and dread of yesterday was gone in an instant. Today was a new day. The early August water ran warm and silky on his body. Eddie swam no more than two metres from the dock. He'd have swum out to the middle of the lake and lingered, but there was no time for that. With its eroding stone path down a sharp hill, ever-thickening forest, listing outhouse in the woods, scraggly brush shoreline, this paradise was work. Hard work. He'd been coming here long enough to know how quickly nature reclaimed space and how continuous the work to stake one's territory.

He made his way onto land and up the grassy slope, soaking wet. Even if he had a towel, Eddie wouldn't have bothered drying himself.

The morning business continued. Eggs cooked over an open fire, dishes scrubbed and shelved. Today, Eddie was taking down trees. Several of the surrounding birches and maples had been threatening his shelter for years. They wouldn't survive the winds of the coming winter.

A trip to town was necessary. His chainsaw was empty, and the gasoline in his jerry can had skunked ages ago. Breakfast complete, Eddie organized and gathered some things before heading up the trail. He'd hiked this path so many times, he could navigate it in pitch darkness and not miss a step. Eddie pushed his way through the hills and dips of thick woods.

The rough-cut cedar drive shed sat hidden among towering

white pines where the road ended and the trail began. Eddie took a ring of keys from its place under a nearby rock and unlocked the folding front doors. There was that smell, that familiar scent that excited him every time he entered. Dampness, motor oil, and dust. He pulled back the tarp on what was among the finest automobiles ever made.

Eddie couldn't have been more conspicuous rolling into town in a royal-blue 1972 Rolls-Royce Corniche and a threadbare business suit. But the locals had long ago gotten beyond the notion that his formerly beautiful suits were some sort of misguided self-aggrandizement. He was just Eddie. He didn't own casual clothes. His suits were all-purpose, worn every day.

Cailly wasn't a town as much as an intersection, really. A sleepy little collection of hardscrabble homes, the township office, a liquor outlet, Rhonda's fall-down Mercantile, a pharmacy of sorts, and a gas station. A river running north to south fed little Cailly Lake at the bottom end of town. A pretty stone bridge ran west across the river to a county road. It was twelve or fifteen kilometres out the county road to the big highway south.

Eddie let Merv dispose of the skunked gas from his jerry can. Words were hardly necessary here. Merv knew what was needed. He took the jerry can from Eddie's hands without banter, walked around the back of the crumbling stucco garage, and poured the old gas into a rusty barrel. Merv's Gas & Auto Repair hadn't been a Texaco station in more than four decades, and yet the sign still hung, peeling and faded, the lone gas pump with its flow indicator balls and flip-plate register. Merv rounded the corner, back to serve his customer.

"Nice to see you, Ed."

Eddie was reasonably certain Merv was no more than a few years older than him. But in the sixty or so years he'd known Merv,

Eddie had no recollection of Merv ever looking like anything other than an eighty-year-old man. Nor could he recollect ever seeing Merv in anything other than an oily, olive-green jumpsuit.

"Well, Merv. I'd be grateful if you could fill it. You're a good man."

"See Rhonda when you're done here. She's got mail for you," Merv said as he filled Eddie's jerry can.

"I'll do that. Thanks," said Eddie.

It didn't occur to Eddie to wonder how Merv would know the woman across the road running the all-in-one grocery-mart, convenience shop, and post office would have mail for him. Of course she'd tell Merv that kind of information. People needed to know; Eddie had mail. That's how Cailly worked. Rules or niceties about personal privacy thrown to the wind. For good or bad, it was like that here. A place where togetherness against rugged elements came before whatever urban sensibilities folks might have about keeping their mouths shut or minding their own business.

Eddie's familiar dread began to rise under the August sun. The low simmering anxiety he'd felt for years. He took the jerry can from Merv and loaded it into the trunk, started the Corniche, and drove it ten metres across the road to a spot in front of Rhonda's. The bells jangled as he made his way through the screen door. Eddie surveyed the space. Time-worn hardwood floors, barely lit rack upon rack of plastic water toys, faded beach towels, long since passed snack items, bins of depressed produce, slide-door fridges half-filled with sugary drinks, the smell of unpackaged red licorice and summer. It was at Rhonda's place that Eddie once came upon a package of old fashioned donuts with a cobweb across the centre hole of one of the donuts.

There she was, as always. Dull pantsuit, haggard, perched

on a padded bar stool behind an ancient cash register. Cigarette-yellowed fingers flipping through garish newsprint, gleaning insight about some starlet of dubious celebrity.

"Just a minute, Mr. Novak. I'll get your things."

Rhonda Lumley liked to keep things succinct. Not unpleasant, just brief. Rhonda dispensed with ordinary pleasantries. Hellos and goodbyes reduced to a simple nod.

"Thank you, Rhonda," said Eddie, waiting patiently as she retrieved his envelopes from a plastic bin atop the lengthy oak-and-glass display cabinet that served as a countertop. Eddie released a wearied sigh. This was a routine he knew well.

Did she think he was fooled by her embarrassing pantomime, or was it just some cruel streak she enjoyed inflicting with silent judgment? Rhonda feigned concern for ensuring proper distribution of Edward R. Novak's mail by slowly, theatrically inspecting each of the envelopes and the sender information. One after another depositing them on the cabinet in front of him. Each like some shameful verdict.

The last of the envelopes was laid on the pile, and Eddie made haste taking them. He'd grown tired of the implied debt Rhonda transmitted for simply receiving and holding his mail. In addition to the judgment she dispensed. "G'day, Rhonda," he said as the doorbells jangled behind him on his way out. Anxiety had given way to low-grade irritation as he walked back to the Rolls. How would his circumstances all play out? Whatever annoyance he might have felt with people knowing, or suspecting they knew, his business, his irritation with them paled in comparison to where he found himself.

Eddie lowered the soft-top of the Rolls. He needed sun and wind to immolate and blow away the sharp spears now piled on his passenger seat in six or eight official-looking envelopes. Whatever vicissitudes awaited, Eddie happily drowned himself in the luxury and elegance of the Corniche as it ferried him home. The cracking and gravelled roads of the north were no match for the suspension and engineering of the Rolls-Royce Corniche. No unexpected dip, no flattened roadkill would unsettle a grandee piloting such a work of art. The sun sparkled on Eddie's bristly face and stringy, grey mane. The lapels of his frayed and filthy suit flapped in the wind.

After stowing the Rolls and locking the folding doors behind him, taking his jerry can and mail with him, Eddie made his way along the trail. He told himself the walk would clear his head, let him settle into whatever new reality awaited. New or not, it wouldn't be unexpected. The trail wound its way through thick old-growth forest, patches of scrub brush, a small clearing of bent grass, up the granite outcropping, and finally down the incline to Eddie's quiet lake. Sweating and tired, Eddie arrived and tramped inside. He poured himself a nip of his favourite single malt, Glenfiddich.

Eddie saw no reason to delay what he knew awaited. He placed his drink on the floor beside the recliner, untangled the elastic band holding his mail, and flipped through the envelopes. Mostly past due notices from creditors, who if given the opportunity, Eddie would righteously rebuke for contacting him. The Bankruptcy and Insolvency Act prohibited such contact with a debtor after an assignment in bankruptcy.

Placing the creditor notices and their envelopes in a small basket beside his recliner for later use lighting fires, Eddie got to the crux of it. He opened the first of the final two envelopes.

LAW SOCIETY TRIBUNAL
HEARING DIVISION

Citation: *Law Society of Ontario v. Novak*, 2022
Date: August 3, 2022
Tribunal File No.: 22A 083

Between:

Law Society of Ontario

Applicant

- and -

Edward R. Novak

Respondent

Before: Robert Krupke

Heard: May 17, 2022

Appearances:
Deanna J. Roth for the applicant
Respondent, self-represented

Summary:
Novak – Summary Hearing – Findings of misconduct – Failure to co-operate – Ungovernable – The Panel finds the Respondent

engaged in misconduct, failed to co-operate and is ungovernable; Panel considered disciplinary history, the investigation, and mitigating factors; revocation – licence to practise law; costs awarded – Respondent ordered to pay costs of hearing $3,500.00, investigation $12,370.00.

REASONS FOR DECISION

OVERVIEW

[1] The Law Society of Ontario has made determinations under s. 34(1) of the Law Society Act, RSO 1990, c. L.8, and s. 6.01(1), and s. 33 of the Rules of Professional Conduct as to whether the Respondent committed professional misconduct and/or conduct unbecoming a licensee. Details of the allegations and the Panel's decision are set out below.

THE ALLEGED MISCONDUCT

The Investigation

[2] On or about January 21, 1997, the Respondent was retained by B.T. to prepare and register a Last Will and Testament, at which time the Respondent was also appointed as executor.

[3] On or about October 9, 1998, the Respondent corresponded with B.T., recommending the preparation of a Power of Attorney for the stated purpose of health decisions and incapacity. In an examination interview, the Respondent

concurred that he had met with B.T., whereupon B.T. executed documents making the Respondent her full Power of Attorney.

[4] On or about February 2, 2016, B.T. passed away after suffering from a longstanding health condition.

[5] S.D.T., the complainant in this action, is the son of B.T. Shortly following B.T.'s death, S.D.T. was provided with the Last Will and Testament prepared by the Respondent.

[6] S.D.T. contended in his complaint that he and his by then deceased sister (and/or her two minor children), were the only beneficiaries of his mother's estate. S.D.T. included in his complaint that the Respondent had attached with the Last Will and Testament a Codicil dated December 28, 2015, naming the Respondent as a beneficiary of various assets and personal effects, among them:

1 Sterling Silver Tea Service
1 Biedermeier Recliner Chair
1/3 interest in PH #1, 2682 4th Ave, The Villages, Florida, 32159
1/3 interest in #312 Dunvegan Rd., Toronto, Ontario, M5P 2P6
1 Tiffany Lamp
1 Platinum, Blue Nile 7.75 Carat Diamond Engagement Ring

[7] In early written inquiries from the complainant to the Respondent concerning the Codicil, and the **Redesignation of Beneficiary** on a **Registered Retirement Income Fund**,

the Respondent contended that B.T. had of her own volition requested and signed the Codicil naming him as a beneficiary of her estate, and redesignating him as the sole beneficiary of her RRIF.

[8] When pressed under Panel examination, the Respondent initially indicated that being named as a beneficiary was in lieu of payment for his services. A review of invoices and banking documents provided clear and unequivocal evidence that the Respondent had billed and been paid for the services which he claimed were compensated for by being named in B.T.'s Last Will and Testament. The Respondent failed to provide any rationale as to why B.T. named him as the redesignated beneficiary of her RRIF.

[9] Throughout the entirety of the investigation, including multiple interviews, the Respondent was alternately vague in his answers, deceptive, and at times objectively untruthful.

[10] S.D.T. indicated that the Respondent had over a period of years ingratiated himself with B.T., forming a bond of trust by purporting to share her religious views, political affiliations, and social circle. S.D.T. asserted that none of these things were based in fact or sincerely held positions and were purposeful flattery and posturing to gain the confidence of B.T. The Respondent's claims to the contrary were undermined by his lack of transparency concerning his compensation, his relationship with the deceased, and by his recalcitrant provision of records and documents.

[11] Though not part of the written complaint made to the Law Society, S.D.T. made oral statements to the effect that at one time he discovered evidence that the Respondent may have been sexually active with B.T., who was 79 years old at the time and suffering from arthritis and osteoporosis.

[12] S.D.T. indicated that a neighbour reported seeing the Respondent leaving B.T.'s home at an early morning hour, and that later in the day, when S.D.T. went to check on his mother, he discovered a man's sock and a personal lubricant product in his mother's bathroom. S.D.T. asserted that his mother was not known to use such a product and that she seemed in unusually high spirits that day.

[13] S.D.T.'s written and oral statements were largely supported by independent witnesses, however, the assertion of a sexual liaison between the Respondent and his client was recorded as unproven and did not form part of the decision-making criteria of the Panel.

Contributing Discoveries

[14] The Panel is obligated to consider the Respondent's potential for causing harm. In the process of investigating the complaint, the investigator uncovered separate practice irregularities. The investigator obtained sworn 3rd party written and oral statements concerning the habitual conduct and comportment of the Respondent. The discovery of items constituting sanctionable professional misconduct include, but are not limited to:

Failure to maintain orderly financial books and records
Refusal or inability to repatriate retainer amounts after a client withdrawal
Sexual impropriety with a junior associate lawyer
Disorderly conduct vis-à-vis public intoxication
Repeated failures to appear for client hearings, trials, and other court proceedings
Failure to remit Employee Source Deductions and Harmonized Sales Tax
Chronic non-payment of creditor invoices
Refusal to transfer documents to new counsel after being discharged from a file
Being the subject of a peace bond with an opposing counsel
Purposefully misdirecting a new Crown Counsel to an incorrect Court location
Feigning illness in order to delay a court proceeding
Leaving confidential client files in the washroom of a drinking establishment

[15] Thorough adjudication of complaints includes document retrieval and analysis, presence or absence of mitigating circumstances, as well as interviews and statements from complainants, involved 3rd parties, and others to whom the Respondent is known. The Panel accepts that contributing discoveries and other apparent issues of conduct and character are not the subject of the complaint. Notwithstanding this, the Panel has an obligation to protect the public.

Disciplinary History

[16] In formulating its decision, the Panel considered the

Respondent's lengthy disciplinary history, as well as evidence pertaining to the Respondent's more recent professional conduct, his reluctant participation in the investigation, obstructive and rude treatment of the investigator, tardy and incomplete provision of documents, misleading answers under questioning, and generally poor co-operation with the Panel.

[17] Adjudication also includes consideration of the Respondent's prior disciplinary matters. The Tribunal's available disciplinary records are limited to those compiled since the establishment of electronic record keeping. Any earlier disciplinary matters memorialized in print form are not included herein and were noted by the Panel but not reviewed as part of this complaint process. A search of the Tribunal's electronic and archived records pertaining to the Respondent included the following:

*Law Society of Upper Canada ("LSUC") renamed Law Society of Ontario – Jan. 1, 2018.

    i.   (1973) Conduct Unbecoming, LSUC Tribunal; records unavail.
   ii.   (1975) Record Keeping, LSUC Tribunal; records unavail.
  iii.   (1976) Illicit Gaming, Contempt of Court, LSUC Tribunal; records unavail.
  iv.   (1976) Traffic Violations, Interference in an Investigation, LSUC Tribunal; records unavail.
   v.   (1976) Possession of an Illegal Substance, LSUC Tribunal; records unavail.

vi. (1981) Disorderly Conduct in a House of Worship, LSUC Tribunal; records unavail.
vii. (1983) Public Intoxication/Urination, LSUC Tribunal; records unavail.
viii. (1984) Conflict of Interest, LSUC Tribunal; records unavail.
ix. (1987) Defecation on colleague's desk, LSUC Tribunal; 6-month suspension, fine, plus costs
x. (1989) Refusal to Co-operate, LSUC Tribunal; 12-month suspension, fine, plus costs
xi. (1990) Practise While Suspended, LSUC Tribunal; extended suspension, fine, plus costs
xii. (1993) Misleading the Court, LSUC Tribunal; 6-month suspension, fine
xiii. (1994) Failure to Maintain Books and Records, LSUC Tribunal; 3-month suspension, fine
xiv. (1996) Abuse of a Court Official, LSUC Tribunal; 3-month suspension, fine
xv. (1996) Failure to Pay Fine, LSUC Tribunal; mandatory bond, educational retraining
xvi. (1998) Mishandling Funds, LSUC Tribunal; 3-month suspension, fine
xvii. (2003) Failure to Appear at a Court Proceeding, LSUC Tribunal; 1-month suspension
xviii. (2005) Unnecessary Litigation, LSUC Tribunal; 1-month suspension
xix. (2009) Mishandling Funds, LSUC Tribunal; Prohibited from Operating Trust Accounts, fine
xx. (2011) False Documents, LSUC Tribunal; mandatory remedial counselling, 2-week suspension

xxi. (2013) Intemperate Language, LSUC Tribunal; reprimand
xxii. (2015) Coercive Behaviour, LSUC Tribunal; reprimand
xxiii. (2017) Public Statements Unbecoming, LSUC Tribunal; reprimand
xxiv. (2018) Conduct Unbecoming, Indecent Exposure, Law Society Ontario; dismissed

Mitigating Factors

[18] In deliberating Mr. Novak's fate, the Panel reviewed and considered his many notable precedent-setting litigation victories in the area of criminal and civil liberties law. Among them:

Mohawk Band v. Archdiocese of Kingston (1974) SCC
Feldstein v. Upper Canada Golf and Country Club (1977) OSCJ
Topless Tropicana Inc. v. Attorney General Province of Ontario (1981) OSCJ
Go-Go Boys Male Review v. Toronto Police Services (1983) OCA
Cabbagetown Disability Collective v. Archibald Properties Inc. (1985) OSCJ
Northern Lakes Preservation Association v. Kingfisher Mines Inc. (1987) SCC
Longworth v. Children's Aid Society Ontario (1987) OSCJ
Buddy's Adult Toys Ltd. v. Town of Keswick (1989) OSCJ

Mr. Novak made a single written representation that his

numerous litigation victories in the areas of criminal and civil law were sufficient grounds to support his continued licensure. While Mr. Novak's contribution to advancement of jurisprudence in these areas was acknowledged, the Panel was not persuaded that his contributions outweighed the requirement for ethical and professional conduct.

Panel's Decision

[19] Despite great effort to work co-operatively with Mr. Novak, he has consistently demonstrated an inability or unwillingness to operate at or within the standard of conduct necessary for members of the Law Society. Since his admission to the bar in 1972, Mr. Novak has been a continuing embarrassment to the profession. In a career spanning nearly 50 years, he has amassed no fewer than 24 separate disciplinary actions. The decision to disbar Mr. Novak is tragic but necessary. His incorrigible behaviour, intemperate and at times profane abuse of clients, judges, juries, court officials, other lawyers, and members of numerous disciplinary panels has made his continued licensure impossible. Despite his encyclopedic knowledge of case law and talent for compelling, often erudite advocacy, he has brought disgrace to the profession. Repeated efforts by the Law Society to channel Mr. Novak's keen intellect toward a more focused and ethical approach to his practice has been unsuccessful. Financial penalties ($62,178.29), suspensions, reprimands, corrective retraining, and professional counselling have proven ineffective in remediating his conduct. Mr. Novak was

given the opportunity to present other members of the bar to speak on his behalf in support of his continued licensure. He was unable to do so.

Order:

[20] It is alleged and demonstrated that contrary to the Rules of Professional Conduct, the Respondent acted without integrity, used undue influence over his client, coerced a benefit disproportionate and unrelated to proper compensation, caused financial injury to legitimate beneficiaries, and generally conducted himself disgracefully. The Tribunal concludes that the Respondent has not met the standard of conduct necessary for continued licensure.

[21] The Respondent is ordered to pay $3,500.00 hearing cost, and $12,370.00 investigation cost.

[22] License to practise is revoked. Edward R. Novak is disbarred from the practice of law in the Province of Ontario, effective August 3, 2022.

Eddie let it all sink down, lit a cigarette, and placed the letter on the ever-growing pile of kindling paper. The long-expected outcome had arrived. The problem was, The Law Society just wouldn't listen. They'd never listened. Not to any of his perfectly plausible explanations for whatever frivolous or minor transgressions he'd been accused of. Yes, there had been occasions along the way when he'd behaved in ways that may not have reflected admirably on himself, but really, what true harm had come to anyone other than himself?

The assertion that his former client had not willingly and of her own desire made Eddie a beneficiary was poppycock. Of course she had. Eddie was a trusted adviser whose counsel had saved her from all manner of predators over the years. His free counsel concerning her divorce from a shipping magnate was masterful. The list of demands he'd prepared right off the top of his head had established her with financial security for the rest of her natural days. She was simply showing her gratitude. Appropriate gratitude in fact. Eddie was far too gentlemanly to even respond to her son's wild accusation of an inappropriate relationship between solicitor and client. The very notion was scandalous. And besides, if a client notifies a solicitor that the solicitor-client relationship is over, then the solicitor-client relationship is terminated. Obviously, the relationship may be resumed later, in some situations within hours, or even minutes.

The constant repetition of ancient contraventions—or alleged contraventions—was proof positive of the tribunal's incessant vindictiveness and unwillingness to let bygones be bygones. They had in every case, after his seventh or eighth complaint, promoted an unfair and inaccurate narrative about Edward R. Novak. On multiple occasions, inflammatory terms like *chronic offender* and *habitual miscreant* had been used.

Yes, there were rare occasions when Eddie had not behaved with the kind of decorum he'd have liked. But there was critically missing nuance to much of it. The illicit gaming, for example, was not as it seemed. Eddie conceded that being a found-in at a gaming den had not been indicative of sagacious decision-making. But really, he was there at the exhortation of a client who'd run afoul of the den's proprietor. Eddie simply wanted to investigate the workings of the establishment; to gain experiential knowledge about how their system of credit and debt collection functioned. Surely a certain level of participation is required to fully understand how it all worked. He'd given clear and detailed statements attesting to how he himself had suffered the proprietor's predatory interest rates. In this case, was Edward R. Novak not the real victim?

Regarding the repeated assertions of disorderly books and records. The answer to such scurrilous accusations was simple. Painfully simple in fact. Eddie presented medical evidence of a movement disorder that caused tremors in his hands, at least one of which he used to prepare billing ledgers and other financial documents. The condition often made him render numbers other than precisely what they should be. Indicative of the Law Society's narrow, mean-spirited approach, they had rejected his doctor's professional correspondence, arguing that Dr. Mbotombe Kwakekemae of Madingou, Republic of the Congo was not a licensed clinician in the Province of Ontario.

As to the allegations of intemperate language and abuse of litigants and various officers of the court including judges, opposing counsel, juries, bailiffs, stenographers, janitorial staff etc., Eddie had indeed on occasion used informal language. But in several of these instances, there had been absurd, perhaps even purposeful, misinterpretations of things he'd said. In one jury trial, documentary evidence revealed a lengthy list of unusual bank deposits by one of Eddie's female clients. The woman had allowed a number of unfortunate but attractive women to take up residence in her home where various male guests would often visit. When it became demonstrably clear that the jury was not siding with his client, his final salutation to them included the phrase, "Bless your hearts, go forth you children of God." Thereafter came the completely perplexing, unfair, and unwarranted Law Society complaints and ensuing opprobrium. Consistent with the Law Society's targeted mistreatment of him, the panel in that case stated that his comment was most definitely not meant in its literal sense and that Eddie's breathless mystification concerning the matter was disingenuous. Yet another unreasonably biased determination against him.

As if it weren't enough having to manage the ceaseless administrative persecutions of the Law Society, the grievous reputational damage resulting from their hounding was considerable. Referencing historic accusations of public intoxication and urination was a bridge too far. The panel on that complaint refused to hear evidence that his conducting of late-night baptisms in the fountains of University Avenue had all been in fun and intended as a sort of tongue-in-cheek Christianizing of the Pagan Summer Solstice holiday. The public urination episode was arguably dismissible on the grounds that the act had taken place in the relative privacy of an alleyway, out of plain view, behind a dumpster. The panel obstinately refused to hear the facts. His torment was unabating.

Among the panel's most egregious overreaches was the unnecessary reference to Eddie's defecation on the desk of a colleague. He had, in fact, defecated, however, mitigating factors were prejudicially ignored.

Eddie lit a du Maurier and took a long drag. A smile crossed his face. He tried to recall whether he'd replaced the chain on his chainsaw last spring as he'd planned. For the life of him, he couldn't remember. The battered old yellow Pioneer P39 was antique at this point. He remembered his own father using it in the 1960s, possibly earlier. Eddie conducted a quick mental inventory of the trees that needed to come down and how he'd drop them. The safe felling of trees was all about angles. Eddie might have been a revered logger in another life. He brought his first tree down when he was nine years old and had been doing it with the precision of a virtuoso since he was twelve. It was the kind of test Eddie favoured. Trees didn't move when approached. Cuts in certain spots, at certain angles, at certain depths would drop a tree exactly where he wanted it. It was art and science he was made for. Eddie opened the last of the envelopes.

| Government | Gouvernement |
| of Canada | du Canada |

Office of the Superintendent
of Bankruptcy

Edward R. Novak
PO Box 34
Station Main
Cailly, Ontario
P0A 1R0

August 4, 2022

Attention: Edward R. Novak
Re: Bankruptcy File # 426915T-2019

Dear Mr. Novak,

You are hereby notified of the final discharge of **Horowitz & Co., Licensed Insolvency Partners Inc.**, 77 Overdale Blvd., Ste. 210, Toronto, ON, M4K 0B6.

Further to your assignment in bankruptcy dated March 31, 2019, you are now an undischarged bankrupt without administration. **Horowitz & Co., Licensed Insolvency Partners Inc.**, sought administrative discharge from file # 426915T-2019, on July 6, 2022, and was granted final discharge on August 4, 2022.

The Trustee's Application for Administrative Discharge was sought on the following bases:

Bankrupt refused to complete 2 mandatory counselling sessions

Bankrupt failed to appear for debtor examinations
Bankrupt failed to remit statutory payments required under the Bankruptcy and Insolvency Act
Bankrupt failed to provide income/expense/asset/liability information
Bankrupt's discharge was opposed by the following proven creditors:

Canada Revenue Agency
Law Society of Ontario
McVety's Tavern Ltd.
Dundurn Internet Cable Co.
Bank of Barbados Visa
St. Leonard's Contracting Ltd.
Morveth Auto Repair Ltd.
David J. Lamphier
City of Dunedin, Florida -Traffic Enforcement Authority
Miller, Walker & Novak Law Partners LLP
Estate of Berenice Thomson (c/o Stephen D. Thomson)
One Stop Mortgage Inc.
King Edward Steakhouse Ltd.
Top Lux Hotel & Casino Las Vegas Nevada Ltd.
Playtime Fantasy Escorts Inc.

<u>Trustee's Report</u>

The original Trustee of Record in your bankruptcy, Daisy Pang BA MBA LIT, was removed from your file on April 7, 2019, due to your behaviour and comments during a meeting held on that date. Ms. Pang cited your persistent references and allusions to her breasts and other parts of her anatomy. Her notes indicate that you smelled of alcohol and appeared intoxicated in your meeting. When a request was made to cease and desist, you continued.

The trustee reported feeling uncomfortable in your presence and requested transfer of your file.

Your file was transferred to Duane Milligan BA JD LIT. Mr. Milligan prepared and submitted the Application for Administrative Discharge on behalf of **Horowitz & Co**.

The application report detailed numerous unsuccessful attempts to contact you via telephone, e-mail, registered mail, and the website of your former law firm. As a condition of bankruptcy, you are required to remain in contact with and available to your trustee. At the request of opposing creditors, Mr. Milligan conducted an investigation and research into your whereabouts and business dealings.

Third-party sources provided anecdotal information pertaining to undisclosed assets and/or monies. Notably, Mr. Milligan's report included numerous witness accounts of you in possession of what is believed to be a 1971, 1972, or 1973, Rolls-Royce Corniche, Licence Plate #AYPW 724. A Motor Vehicle Registry search of the plate appears to confirm a Wanda Josephine Trudell as registrant. Retaining undisclosed beneficial ownership of an asset is a serious offence under the Bankruptcy and Insolvency Act (R.S.C. 1985, c. B-3).

An Ontario Provincial Police media release indicates that a person matching your description was questioned on suspicion of driving under the influence, standing in close proximity to a vehicle of the same make and model, on July 23, 2021, in the parking area of Hidey-Hole Storage Rental Ltd., at approximately 2:27 a.m., in Gravenhurst, Ontario.

On January 17, 2020, Mr. Milligan contacted the phone number listed on your bankruptcy intake sheet. He left a recorded message requesting a return phone call. On January 18, 2020, he received a phone call from you. During that call, you indicated that you would be forwarding all previously requested financial documents. The material was never provided. The telephone call display indicated a 352 area code. This area code is known to serve the community of The Villages and surrounding region in the State of Florida. A reverse search of the phone number associated the number to the address: PH #1, 2682 4th Ave, The Villages, Florida, 32159. A search of the Florida Land Records and Deeds Directory lists the property owners as Stephen Douglas Thomson and Madison Maureen Thomson (In Trust), jointly with Tyler Marcus Thomson (In Trust), and Edward R. Novak. You are required to disclose or report worldwide income and/or assets. Failure to disclose worldwide income and/or assets is a serious offence under the Bankruptcy and Insolvency Act (R.S.C. 1985, c. B-3).

On or about February 23, 2020, in person interviews were conducted at the Toronto Dominion Bank, 107 North Kinton Avenue, Huntsville, ON, P1H 0A9. Staff at the branch confirmed that on multiple occasions you used a Power of Attorney document to obtain access to a safety deposit box registered to Mrs. Laura McAllister, RR 1, Station A, Dorsett, Ontario, P1L 0B4. Under the Powers of Attorney Act, (R.S.O. 1990 c. P.20) undischarged bankrupt persons are not permitted to act as Power of Attorney. Once a bankrupt individual has received an unconditional discharge, they may apply (or reapply) to act as Power of Attorney.

Mr. Milligan's report details a list of creditors from whom you obtained credit, supplies, or services during the period March 31,

2019, through and including June 28, 2022. Various individuals and commercial enterprises declined or were unable to provide documents or statements pertaining to dealings with you. The following parties did provide written undertakings and/or signed applications for credit bearing your signature:

Air North Charter – Credit Granted	($7,916.32)
Wild North Golf & Country – Credit Granted	($2,803.96)
Gravenhurst Landscape Supply – Credit Granted	($3,362.41)
Muskoka Summerwinds Resort – Credit Granted	($ 973.09)
Muskoka Family Fun Houseboat Rentals – Credit Granted	($ 772.46)

The above noted parties provided sworn statements that you failed to notify them of your bankruptcy status prior to obtaining credit. Bankrupt persons are required to notify potential creditors of an ongoing undischarged bankruptcy. Failure to do so is a serious offence under the Bankruptcy and Insolvency Act.

Documentary evidence provided by several commercial enterprises in the City of Toronto included signed credit card receipts with a credit card available through Bank of Britain, domiciled on the islands of St. Kitts and Nevis. The card and receipts appear to bear your name. No such credit instrument appears on your Statement of Affairs. Bankrupt persons are required to disclose all credit cards. Failure to do so is a serious offence under the Bankruptcy and Insolvency Act.

The Trustee's report enumerates various unsuccessful attempts to contact or engage you in resolving your bankruptcy. You may seek readministration with another Trustee by contacting our office and providing the information that was requested in correspondences dated April 23, 2019; August 11, 2019; October 3, 2019; February 8, 2020. You will be required to submit to sworn debtor examinations concerning any bank accounts held in your name, holdings or assets held in your name or to your benefit or use, credit you may have obtained during the period of your bankruptcy, currency (domestic or foreign) you may be in possession of, objects and items of value in your possession, real property you may be holding or using and that are held in trust for you by others. You will be required to attend two mandatory counselling sessions. You will remain an undischarged bankrupt until such time as these conditions are met.

Sincerely,

Maria Saldanas BA LIT
Case Manager
Investigations Division
Office of the Superintendent
of Bankruptcy
151 Yonge St., 4th Floor,
Toronto, ON
M5C 2W7

Eddie took a slow sip. Enough to warm his chest with the comfort of his single malt Scotch. He had spent a lifetime in its succour. Win or lose it had been there for him at the end of each and every trial. Often in the middle of them. Problematically so, at times. In the pricey steakhouses and low-light watering holes favoured by downtown litigators, it wasn't unusual to hear of Eddie's legendary, midtrial, nocturnal exploits. Certainly, there were trials that ended in tears for his clients. Trials where he had infuriated judges and juries by arriving late, dishevelled, malodorous, incoherent. Where he'd struggled to form a cogent sentence, spewing irrelevant, circuitous nonsense. But there was a reason Eddie was permitted to carry on as long as he had. There was a reason his antics had been indulged. Edward R. Novak practised no more than eighteen months before word spread about the brilliant young lawyer who'd arrived with the wisdom of Socrates and the eloquence of a poet.

In his finest moments, Eddie left judges and juries spellbound, speechless, awestruck. Lawyers working unrelated cases in whatever courthouse Eddie was appearing in began crashing the gates for seats at his trials. Soon after, lawyers from other parts of the city, in other areas of law. Then lawyers from out of town began demanding access to watch him weave rhetorical spells. Court reporters struggled to describe the word magic they had witnessed. Edward R. Novak LLB was a glittering spectacle of articulation and argumentation. His gift for articulating the most arcane and esoteric legal principles, with pristine clarity, was otherworldly. His command of case law, devastating.

For Edward R. Novak, a trial was about that moment; that one imperceptibly brief moment when an electrical current ran through him like lightning; the hair on the back of his neck stood on end, and he knew in every cell of his body, he had won. It was that instant whether on cross, or closing statements, and even on rare occasions in opening statements, when Edward R. Novak LLB, took flight. It happened with enough regularity in the early days, he began to hunt it. When that moment came, he would stride with confidence to his seat, lean in to his client, and tell them, it was over. He was never wrong when he felt it. Not once. So palpable, so real in its intensity, he chased that moment in dreams. Eddie would begin with apologies to the judge and jury for the inconvenience of their having to participate in such proceedings. He would assure them he was aware of the need for brevity, then crack wise at his own expense. Usually about some peculiarity of his appearance. Laughter was a judge or jury's tell. They were on his side. He would launch, and the show would begin. When Edward R. Novak began persuasive speech, his word choice, tone, inflection, vocabulary, cadence, and rhythm were an irresistible force of eloquence. Before all else, above all else, Edward R. Novak was a master storyteller. Whatever deformities of character Eddie might have were microscopic in the shadow of his artistry.

Once a judge or jury had shown their tell, Eddie went to work picking apart the opposition's position through inference, imagery, reason, philosophical erudition, recitations of case law, folksy patter, allegory, metaphor, fable. With every syllable, at every turn, his facility with language and mellifluous voice overwhelmed. People liked Eddie. They wanted him to win. In full flight, he was unmatched. A performer so good, he drew crowds. Edward R. Novak strode the boards of a courtroom like a stage actor, drawing his audience into an intimacy so compelling, it became a love story. He would engage his prey, reroute the pathways of their minds, inspire their spirits, whisper in their ears, seize their hearts, make them heroes in the story he was telling. With an epic poem he would carry them safely across pitching waters. He would conclude with oratory so incontrovertible, so crushing, judges and juries were powerless under his spell. With his final sentence, final word, final breath, Edward R. Novak delivered his story with unassailable authority. And then, motionless, he would wait. Standing alone before them in their awestruck, hypnotized silence, he would for that one brief moment, transcend the world of mortals, and become a God.

Chapter 2

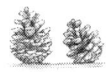

The correspondence Eddie received laid him low for three days. Yes, he had little regard for the decrees and concerns of the Law Society, the Superintendent of Bankruptcy, his former trustee, and in a way, his creditors, but still, to be stripped of one's law licence and officially stuck in bankruptcy was dispiriting.

Several rotting birches and maples now felled, trunks sectioned, limbs removed and stacked on the burn pile, chainsaw turned off, Eddie removed the small wads of toilet paper lodged in his ears and stopped for a short rest. His mind lingered on the notes playing in his head. Debussy's final D-flat at the close of "Clair de Lune." Was it D-flat? Yes, but what about it? Something. Eddie lit a du Maurier and wondered in the sun.

Three more trees came down with deadly precision. Exhausted, Eddie called it quits. It was long past time for a drink. He stripped off his wingtip brogues, bespoke pinstriped suit, and pit-stained dress shirt and piled them by the door. In the kitchenette, tilting bottle to mouth, naked and thirsty, he swallowed the last ounces of Scotch whisky. Time for a dip. He made his way down to the lake. Wading in from the sandy shoreline beside the dock, he lingered ankle-deep in the shallows before marching forward and plunging under.

In the middle of the uninhabited lake, Eddie savoured the heat of the sun on his back. Treading water, he surveyed the shoreline as far as his head would turn to either side. He took it all in. Dense forest, the areas of tall grass along the northern edge, the deep bay across the lake cluttered with driftwood, pink granite cliffs east across the water, the smooth rock shore to the south. With a deep breath, he allowed himself to sink below the surface. A purposeful descent until he could no longer feel the sun-warmed water of the surface. It was cooler down below. The relief he longed for. Cool, silent, amniotic.

Ashore, renewed, Eddie hauled himself onto the dock, stood for a moment, and dried in the sun. Water dripped and evaporated from his body: his spindly legs, pendulous testicles, paunchy belly, sagging chest and arms, at their brownest now from six weeks of summer sun. Eddie retrieved his cassette player from the shelf inside the screened-in porch. He pawed through the basket of tapes beside the player. Today was a day for Brahms rhapsodies.

Eddie placed the tape player beside him on the dock and lay down. Fresh batteries at the ready, sun rays warming him, gentle ripples lapping in the shore grass, a quiet Brahms rhapsody. Thoughts, visions, sensations filling him, Eddie drifted into space. Thick-cut prime rib, red wine rosemary jus, roast carrot with fennel, sauteed mushrooms over polenta. Lavender crème brûlée, warm single malt. His wife Judith, naked, outstretched, waiting. The heft and roundness of her breasts. His wife Denise and her magnificent bottom. His secretary paramour, Susan, how wet and ravenous she'd been behind his desk. The velvet supple thighs of his lifelong friend and lover, Lorna. The many nameless women he'd known in foreign lands. Nights of hashish, opium, Russian vodka.

The morning passed, and he could no longer stand the hunger making his stomach grumble. Eddie roused himself from the dock and made for the kitchenette. Too hungry for the complications of bread, tomato, mustard, Eddie gnawed on a leg of chicken, enough to stop the wolves within. After a cigarette and some water, he organized himself for a trip to the liquor outlet. He pulled apart the pile of clothes by his bed, quickly locating his cleanest dirty pants and shirt. He dressed and closed the door behind him on his way out. The trail was as green and lush as it had ever been. Who might he meet along the way? Eddie lived among the bear, coyote, and wolf.

The journey was longer today. Over an hour. His breath more laboured. It was the heat and humidity. It must be. Winded, Eddie arrived at the top of the hill and leaned on a tree by the rock where he kept the key ring. He smoked a du Maurier and rested a moment. Still in the lingering ecstasy of Brahms, it occurred to him what a scourge big band music had been to the world, with its loathsome uptempo bugles, trumpets, and percussive noise.

Pushing back the folding doors of the drive shed, Eddie took a stepladder from a hook behind the Rolls. He spread its legs and ascended to the top, where he reached for the metal lockbox resting on a sheet of plywood laid upon the rafters above him. Eddie lowered himself carefully. Finding a tiny key among the others on the ring, he opened the box and removed a handful of fifty-dollar bills. Folding the bills and placing them in his pocket, he locked the box and returned it to its spot.

Eddie drove slowly, taking in the majesty of the Canadian Shield on a summer day, with its verdant rolling hills, sweeping panoramas, rivers, and streams. The liquor outlet was busy today. Residents and cottagers all looking for their spirits in anticipation of the weekend regatta held on Cailly's own little lake.

Eddie wasted no time chatting or catching up with familiar locals. He was there for single malt Scotch, not friend-making. Retail purchasing was uncomfortable territory for Eddie. Cash and carry only. The separation of money from his hands. He watched carefully as the strapping young lad at the till counted off change from a hundred cash.

Cigarettes were needed. Eddie thought for a moment about the distance from the liquor outlet to the Mercantile. Not exactly across the street but not far enough to drive. He placed his bottles on the passenger-side floor of the Rolls and walked. The overhead bells jangled as Eddie entered through the screen door. Plump, impassive Rhonda greeted him from her perch behind the oak cabinet.

"Eddie."

"Hello, Rhonda."

"Whatta you need?" she asked.

"Du Maurier, large. Two please," said Eddie. It remained a curiosity to him that she had to ask, after thirteen years of selling him the same cigarettes, in the same quantity.

"Thirty-one eighty," she said, needlessly. Eddie was well aware of the cost of cigarettes. Passing her a new fifty-dollar bill, he watched closely as she counted off his change.

"Your bulb came in," said Rhonda.

"Ah, excellent. Thank you, madam. I appreciate the notice," said Eddie.

"Merv said to tell you to come when you're ready," she responded.

"I'll do that, thank you." The prospect of not having to repeat a trip into town pleased him. He'd pop over presently and have Merv replace the extinguished bulb in his driver's-side tail lamp. He'd wait if he had to, but that seemed unlikely. Merv was habitually immediate in his service. Merv had long ago proven his worth. Shortly after Eddie came to possess the Rolls and after two or three minor repairs, Merv had established his value by notifying Eddie that he'd ordered the operator's manual for the 1972 Rolls-Royce Corniche in anticipation of future repairs. This seemed to Eddie an indication of uncommon intelligence. He appreciated that.

"See you again, Rhonda," said Eddie, his words scarcely raising an eyebrow from her. The bells still jangling as he exited the screen door, Eddie narrowly avoided walking squarely into Town Councillor Stephen Coutts, who was on his way into the Mercantile. With a nod and smile, Stephen greeted him.

"Steve," Eddie responded with perfunctory dispatch.

"Stephen," Stephen corrected.

"Right," Eddie replied.

"Murray and Jeff said they heard your chainsaw goin' when they were up the hydro line," said Stephen.

"Congratulate them for me," said Eddie.

"Tree removal bylaw says you need a permit for trees on township property," said Stephen.

"Does it?" asked Eddie with feigned surprise.

"If you're takin' trees down on township property, along the shoreline anyway, you need a permit." Eddie glimpsed a faint smile crossing Stephen's face.

"It escaped my notice that there was a tree shortage in the boreal forest," said Eddie, folding his arms and cocking his head.

"I'm just tellin' you," said Stephen.

"I see. Correct me if I'm wrong. You were elected to Cailly Town Council, is that right?"

"Three times running," said Stephen bristling with confidence.

"Right, and as far as I know, the lot I'm on is in Perry Township. Are you a member of that council too?" Eddie asked.

"Well, no, but—"

Eddie interrupted, "And you've taken it upon yourself to act as a kind of information kiosk for them. Good for you, Steve."

"Stephen."

"Of course. Yes. Well, look," said Eddie, "apart from the fact that the trees on the waterfront I occupy are outside your purview, unless and until you're in possession of evidence that a tree has been removed in contravention of the township's alleged bylaw, I'd appreciate very much if you'd mind your own business."

"They can come and check," said Stephen, threatening.

"Interesting. You realize the Township of Perry doesn't have a 'tree removal bylaw,' right?" asked Eddie.

"Sorry to tell you, I'm pretty sure they do," said Stephen with a withering smile.

Eddie addressed the matter directly. "It's called 'Vegetative Buffers,' and you'll find it in section 3.29 of the Zoning Act. Specifically, what you'll find it says is, 'Where there is the shoreline of a lake or watercourse on or appurtenant to a lot, a vegetative buffer of thirty metres shall be maintained between all buildings and structures and the shoreline or watercourse. This buffer may be interrupted for a width of ten percent of the shoreline frontage of the lot to provide for a pathway to the water.' No doubt this was all uppermost in your mind when you issued your . . . 'caution,' let's call it. And without boring you terribly, a permit is not required. Arrangements of this sort are addressed in a zoning agreement," said Eddie with the finality of death.

"Well, I . . . I'm . . . I'm . . . sure you . . . I'm just. Just sayin', Eddie."

"Fuck off, Steve. Excuse me. Fuck off, Stephen." With that, Eddie smiled and sauntered back up the road to retrieve the Rolls-Royce Corniche.

Eddie barely had the Rolls stopped before Merv was out on the lot, bulb in hand.

"G'day Ed," said Merv.

"Greetings, Mervin. Thanks for this. You're a sage and a prince among men," said Eddie.

"Ten minutes with it," Merv responded. Eddie had time to kill. Leaving the work to Merv, Eddie wandered down to the little lake upon whose shores the Town of Cailly sat. He strolled the park with its public beach where children swam. Where the community would hold its annual regatta that very weekend, and where he himself had swum, seventy years ago. Much had happened in his life between then and now. He'd gone through elementary and secondary school, undergraduate, and law school, married, divorced, married again, had a child, travelled to dozens of countries, spent fifty years practising law, and here he was. Right back where he started.

Eddie looked across the water and thought of a time so many years earlier. A time of confusion and haste, drama and dread. He'd brought his daughter here forty-one years ago. Eddie had spent a full day in this park with Melanie, helping her up the steps of the slide, holding her as she swung from the climbing bars, taking her in the water on his back as she clung to his neck, floating her in the waves. His angelic wife, Denise, had vacated the matrimonial home with Melanie twenty-two months after their marriage. They'd been married quietly at City Hall when she was eight months pregnant after his lightning-quick divorce from Judith. Access to Melanie was allowed that particular day more out of necessity than generosity. Denise was having surgery, a therapeutic hysterectomy, and needed several days to recuperate. It was arranged that Eddie would be allowed to take Melanie to his midtown Toronto home where they were to stay until Denise's surgical wounds had settled. It was made clear it would be no longer than two nights.

Eddie saw this brief custody as an opportunity to introduce his daughter to the north, the land, and the lake that had been so formative from the earliest days of his own life. Unthinking, he'd failed to inform Denise, or anyone for that matter, that he would be taking Melanie from the city.

The morning of the second day of Denise's recovery, she'd phoned Eddie from her apartment in the west end of Toronto. Unable to reach him by phone on the evening of the first night, nor the morning of the second day, and generally panicked as to the whereabouts of her daughter, according to the messages she'd left, Denise had taken it upon herself to go to Eddie's in an attempt to find them. Fragile from poorly conducted abdominal surgery, Denise had dressed and walked to the subway station. The train was barely two stations from her High Park entry point before Denise's stitches had ripped and the internal sutures had ruptured. Well before arriving at Yonge St. station, Denise lay hemorrhaging on the floor of a moving train. Denise gave up this life seconds before ambulance attendants could provide professional medical care.

The aftermath of Denise's passing was fraught with anger and recrimination. Eddie had made the unwise calculation of proposing a reconciliation with Judith. His pitch had been that the love affair leading to Melanie's conception, his parting with Judith, and the eventual marriage to Denise were small considerations in the face of Melanie's desperate need for a mother and stable family. Judith would have none of it. Meanwhile, Denise's mother, Theresa; and sister, Angela, residents of Casper, Wyoming, had come to Toronto.

Being greeted at the airport by several of Denise's close

friends, the two were quickly made aware of Eddie's reputation as a philanderer and general louse. As a matter of thoroughness, the pair were provided with newspaper accounts filled with inferences to Eddie's drug- and alcohol-fuelled bacchanalia at various discotheques and nightclubs. Some included pictures. The eventual and inevitable confrontations and ensuing round of mutually screamed threats between Eddie, Theresa, and Angela left Eddie in a quandary.

He could insist on continued custody of Melanie, not ideal without a responsible adult to care for the child, or he could surrender custody to Denise's mother and sister. Game as Eddie might have been to take his child without the assistance of a wife or girlfriend, Denise's younger sister made clear that she'd litigate for custody and make a point of providing the court with ample evidence to consider in determining his fitness as a parent. Already the subject of several Law Society complaints, Eddie had no desire to expose himself to more complaints based on publicly reported material and upon which the Law Society might respond with additional reprimands, suspensions, or fines. Theresa and Angela returned to Casper with Melanie in tow.

Eddie's effort to communicate with Melanie in the early years had yielded no response, and his attempts to arrange visitation were aggressively rebuffed. A postcard had arrived six years ago. The content of which revealed precisely nothing about her life or appearance. There was a phone call to him several years later. Some incidental bit of family history Melanie wanted to know. The conversation was respectful but stilted and brief. Eddie was quite certain her mother's family would have coloured Melanie's perspective about him. If not that, then a search of the internet anytime in the preceding twenty years would certainly have yielded a trove of information about him. Most of it unsavoury.

Thirsty and slightly agitated, Eddie returned to Merv's to retrieve the Rolls, get out of town, and back to his lair. He wasn't two or three kilometres outside Cailly before he had his knee on the wheel and his hands on a bottle, removing the cap. Eddie lifted the bottle to his mouth as he drove, resting the bottle in his crotch between sips. Warm single malt, a 1972 Rolls-Royce Corniche convertible, solitude, and the Canadian wilderness. How perfect.

Rolls stowed and locked up, key ring stored, cigarettes and liquor in hand, Eddie began the trek home. The days were beginning to noticeably shorten again, so Eddie wasted no time. He had things to do. The finale of Tchaikovsky's 6th Symphony playing in his head as he followed the trail, Eddie pondered what his daughter might look like. Did she have his nose? Was she as long legged as her father? Did she have her mother's sparkling smile? The one he'd been so enchanted by. Eddie did not know his daughter.

What he would give to see her face. To bring her here. To share this retreat with her. So often he'd wondered who she might be. Driving Highway 400 north, smoking his last cigarette of the night, listening to Liszt's *Liebesträume*, and in a million other circumstances, he'd thought of Melanie.

Where was she? Did she ever think of him? Was she loved by a decent man? A man who treated her with kindness. What was she like as a preteen, an adolescent, a twenty-three-year-old, a thirty-five-year-old? He'd missed all of it. These thoughts surfaced in the stillness of his memory of that perfect, perfect day in the park, forty-one years ago. The police had been called. Denise was taken to St. Michael's Hospital in an ambulance but, by all accounts, was gone by the time she was even put on a gurney. The newspaper reported that the Transit Commission took the subway car out of service to replace the floor and much of the wiring under several seats that were ruined with saturation.

In the frantic search for Melanie, one of Denise's friends recalled Eddie speaking about Cailly. She thought he'd said something about a cabin nearby. She told police, and after finding Cailly on a map, the Toronto Police Service called the Ontario Provincial Police detachment in Burk's Falls, who drove down through Emsdale to notify Eddie. Two older officers and a very fresh-looking younger officer had made their way along the trail to his cabin and found Eddie playing on the floor with Melanie. Their silent approach had caught him off guard when they knocked on the screen door.

"Mr. Novak, do you have a moment?" one of the officers asked.

"I wasn't expecting . . . You've caught me in a bit of a . . ." Eddie said.

"Yes, well, unfortunately, it's important," the young man said. The sight of their uniforms called to Eddie's mind a variety of circumstances and behaviour he may have been involved in.

"Right, okay. Step in." Eddie stood to greet the three officers.

Melanie carried on tapping a wooden spoon on an overturned pot.

"How can I help you, gentlemen?" Eddie asked.

"Well, um, Mr. Novak, um, okay, I should introduce . . . I'm ahh . . . I'm Officer Stan. No. No. Kazubowski. I mean, I'm Stan Kazubowski. Officer Kazubowski. And this is—"

"Ted Davies, Eddie," said the heavier of the two older gentlemen.

"Jim Ferguson," said the taller, thinner of the two. The pair now shifting uncomfortably on their feet.

"Sorry, excuse me, Officer Davies, were we on opposite sides at trial? You look familiar. Have we met?" Eddie asked.

"No. Not in that way. We have met though. I've escorted you home once or twice. Just to the top of the trail anyway," said Ted tucking his cap under his arm.

"Oh, right. Of course. Grateful, thank you, Officer Davies," said Eddie.

"Stan, why don't you fill Mr. Novak in on why we've come this afternoon," said Jim.

"All right then. So, I guess, um. Where should I start? So earlier this afternoon, we got a call from . . . the um . . . Is this your baby?" asked Officer Kazubowski bending ever so slightly.

"Yes, look how can I help you gentlemen today?" asked Eddie.

"Okay, so like I was saying. We got a call today from Toronto. The police there. The Toronto Police. And so. So, this is your cabin, is that right?" asked Officer Kazubowski.

"Stan, what you want to do is just deliver the message as quickly as possible after arrival, okay?" Officer Ferguson instructed patiently.

Eddie looked to Officer Kazubowski and detected a slight quiver on his lower lip.

"Right. Okay. Okay. I'm gonna deliver the . . . yeah. Okay, so, um, Mr. Novak, your wife died this morning. Denise Garland. She's your wife, right? Denise Garland?" Officer Kazubowski blurted.

Stunned but still composed, Eddie reeled a moment. "Ex-wife."

"Ex?" asked Officer Davies.

"She left me," Eddie confirmed.

"We're sorry either way, Eddie," said Officer Ferguson.

"Okay, so . . . you're okay then, or should we . . . ?" Officer Kazubowski inquired.

Seeing the struggle, Eddie looked the young man in the eye.

"You're new," said Eddie.

"He's a young officer, Eddie. We're helping him," said Officer Davies.

Eddie held the young man's gaze. Officer Kazubowski hadn't been on the job more than a week. Eddie took him by the shoulder and spoke firmly and encouragingly.

"You've done well here today. Keep at it." The rest was murky. It all happened so long ago.

Descending the length of hill through the trees down to the cabin, Eddie stashed his cigarettes and liquor and went about his business, cleaning and stacking dishes, storing the chainsaw and axe, washing and then hanging wet shirts and briefs from a tree branch to dry, and finally laying the fire to cook the evening meal: a can of Irish stew.

The sun dipped below the tree line behind him as he spooned the last of the stew into his mouth. Sitting on a cut log by the fire, Eddie poured himself another cup of single malt. His third. It had been a painful week. Eddie lit a du Maurier and smoked in the golden quiet of sunset. The fire crackled, and sparks rose into the darkening sky. Where had it all gone wrong with Denise? And Melanie. He watched the smoke rise into the night and turned his thoughts to Judith. The night they'd met. The weakness he'd felt. Fear even.

It was a summer gala at the Royal Danish Consulate. Eddie was on the invite list because of his work with a Copenhagen-based environmental group. Judith Hansen had only recently arrived in Toronto to work as a document translator for the consulate. Six feet tall, white blond, buxom, fresh faced. Eddie was unsteady on his feet when he met her. Not twenty-one days passed before he'd known Judith beneath the stars on the dock he could now hit with well-aimed spit.

Eddie cried for nine days when Judith left him, only stopping at Denise's insistence, who grew increasingly furious with his histrionics. Far from being embarrassed by his night-time antics and romantic drama playing out in newspaper articles, Eddie was keenly aware that notoriety was every bit as valuable as public acclaim. He made no effort to lower his profile. But like all things, the soap opera of general bad behaviour, licentiousness, and professional misconduct grew tired. Attention shifted, and the press and the public moved on from the Eddie Novak show.

In his first thirty years of practice, Edward R. Novak LLB moved from genius wunderkind to consummate professional . . . to *enfant terrible*, to folk hero, to laughable bozo. The last twenty years had been spent as an embarrassing running joke. It was time to sleep and dream of better days.

As the morning sun rose, Eddie lingered in half-sleep dreams. Górecki's Symphony no. 3 and the sound of rustling trees in a cool wind ushered him awake. He lay motionless, contemplating the music in his head and the sound of wind in the trees. What would he do today? He would read, of course. As he always did. He'd listen to his favourite cassette tapes, Górecki, Purcell, Chopin, Dvorak. He'd swim, chop some wood maybe. He'd go about his business quietly and in solitude.

Eddie rose from his bed, retrieved a du Maurier and his lighter. He went to the edge of the brush behind his cabin and smoked a full cigarette before fully emptying his bladder. A temperamental prostate had become the bane of his existence. He built a small fire in his firepit and returned to the cabin for his breakfast items. Eddie took from his old bar fridge three eggs and a small steak, lifted the ancient skillet from its hook on the wall beside the fridge, and extracted his knife and fork from the cutlery pile. Stepping out into the August air, Eddie placed the skillet on the grill over his fire, fried the steak and eggs, and ate from the pan.

After a passing rinse in the lake, skillet, knife, and fork were placed on the dock. Eddie stripped out of his briefs and plunged into the lake. He swam to the middle and rolled onto his back, floating as well as he could without moving. He took in the cloudless blue sky before allowing himself to sink. Descending into dark, cold silence, he rested as long as his breath would allow before surfacing. Too tired for the front crawl, he side-stroked back to the dock.

Eddie collected his items from the dock and returned to the fire. Jostling the remainder of a few sticks of wood, he conjured enough flame to warm and dry himself. Several hours of reading in his recliner, cigarettes, and a Chopin nocturne followed.

As afternoon drew down, Eddie rummaged his kitchenette shelf for a bag of peanuts and took a seat on the step outside the screened-in porch. He took a handful of peanuts from the bag and cracked and rustled the shells between his fingers. The call was soon enough answered, and his chipmunk friends quickly scampered to his side. They ate from shells held between his toes, then from his open hand. He placed peanuts on his shoulder and encouraged them to run up his arm. Eddie sat feeding his friends and watching them eat.

Nuthatches, sparrows, jays, and finches began to gather in the tree branches. Eddie took peanuts from the shells, broke them up, and tossed them to the base of the trees. There, the birds circled on the ground, pecking and nibbling. In communion with creatures of the wild, he sat in peace. Eddie liked any living thing that didn't talk.

Chapter 3

Eddie rolled into town under grey skies. Cailly was very quiet today. End of August cottagers must have been busy packing up their places. He appreciated the quiet that came with that seasonal exit. Not that their presence affected him at his isolated spot. Nevertheless, on his trips to town, Eddie enjoyed the reduced traffic at Merv's, the liquor outlet, the Mercantile, and the pharmacy. Today's plan was simple. Grab his bottles at the liquor outlet, gas up at Merv's, then retreat to his cabin in the woods.

The liquor outlet was deserted. Eddie made haste, retrieving his bottles in under a minute. The lone employee stood folding boxes beside the cash register. Lanky, bearded Darren McIntyre was a youngish forty-six and lived with his wife Beth in a comfortable two-bedroom apartment above the pharmacy. They came to occupy the apartment by way of Beth's work as the pharmacy technician. The itinerant pharmacist for the area owned the building and had encouraged them to take the apartment. It wasn't a pharmacy in the fullest sense of the word. A dispensary really. Nonetheless, it was a critically important facility in a community with a seniors' residence. The pharmacist owned several other dispensaries and pharmacies in a handful of nearby towns and hamlets. He spent most of his time travelling between them, preparing orders. Pharmacy technicians like Beth did the rest. Darren made a modest but comfortable salary at the liquor outlet and supplemented his income helping locals with small contracting jobs.

They exchanged greetings as Darren moved to ring in Eddie's purchases.

"Quiet here today," said Eddie.

"End of season," said Darren.

"How was the regatta?"

"Good this year. Murray went ass over teakettle into the lake in the first heat of the one-man canoe race. God, we roared. Funniest thing I've ever seen," said Darren, slipping the first bottle into a paper bag.

"Did Melinda cheat, as usual?" Eddie asked.

"'Course she did. Wouldn't be the regatta if she didn't," said Darren.

"Well, she's consistent if nothing else."

"Rhonda was in last night, said to tell you, you've got mail."

"I'm sure she did. Thank you, Darren."

"You too, Eddie."

Eddie stopped at Merv's pump. Merv greeted him from under a car in the garage bay. "Hi, Ed, gimme a minute."

"No rush. I'm across the street for my mail. Fill it, will you please, Merv?" said Eddie over his shoulder as he walked across the road.

"She's not there, Ed," Merv called after him.

"Who?" asked Eddie.

"Rhonda, down to Huntsville about her shoulder. Travis is covering," said Merv.

Eddie made it across the empty road and opened the jangly

bell screen door. He crossed the threshold slowly, taking a moment to survey the scene in its totality. Two of five waist-high produce stands lay on their sides amidst a riot of limp produce strewn hither and yon. Oranges and purple onions, parsnips, squash, and green bananas cluttered the floor among cans of Campbell's soup. Shards of glass from the broken overhead light fixture crunched under his feet. The doors of the refrigerators had been left flung open. A broken bottle of salsa drizzled its contents onto the floor in front of the oak display cabinet where Rhonda kept her roost. Eddie could hear the frenzied crinkling of bags being torn apart, but saw no one.

"Trav?" Eddie called out gently. Met with silence, he called again, "Travis?" Eddie walked slowly around the tall metal stand stacked with bread. Looking down the aisle behind, he found Travis. "Hello, Travis," he said.

Bent at the waist, knees and hips in a spastic spin, arms dangling and swaying from his torso, Travis quickly stood erect from the pile of potato chips and empty bags on the floor in front of him. Jerking and swaying, Travis reached to the shelf in front of him and took a small jar of gherkin pickles, raised his arm, and hurled them at Eddie. The trajectory of the jar being off by several feet, the pickles bounced harmlessly off a large wicker basket of corn. Eddie remained motionless, watching skeletal Travis in his grease-blackened sweatpants and ragged concert T-shirt, the veins in his neck distended, distorting the snakehead tattoo on his throat, facial scabs weeping, track marks lining his tattooed arms.

"Travis, I'm here to pick up my mail," said Eddie.

Travis resumed emptying the potato chip bags onto the floor, possessed by a rolling, spastic dance.

Eddie approached him slowly. "Travis, Viper is under the river bridge. He needs to talk with you," he said quietly and calmly. Travis's eyes grew wide as he warily studied Eddie. "Travis, you should go see Viper now. He's waiting for you."

Travis bolted for the door, pushing Eddie aside on his way. Eddie followed to the wooden inside door, closed and locked it as Travis exited. He watched as Travis jerked and rolled his way up the road to the river bridge. He surveyed what he could see of town through the front window and saw no one. Eddie wasted no time, rapidly moving toward the rear of the shop through the chaos of overturned produce stands, scattered chips, and emptied bags. He walked through to the back hall and firmly locked the rear door before searching out a broom and large garbage bin from under a shelf in the hall. He returned to the shop floor, where he closed the fridge doors.

Righting the produce stands, Eddie piled the fruits and vegetables back into place and returned the soup cans to their places on the metal racks. He made short work of the chips and bags, sweeping them up into the garbage bin along with the broken glass from the overhead light and shattered salsa bottle. Finally, Eddie opened a package of paper towels and wiped up the mess of salsa from the floor in front of the oak display cabinet. He looked the shop over. It wasn't perfect, but it would do. Save for the broken overhead light fixture, no real damage.

Eddie stepped behind the oak display cabinet and opened a small plastic storage bin beside the register. He searched through orderly rows of mail. Finding his name, he took his three envelopes and tucked them into his inside suit jacket pocket. From a shelf on the wall behind the cabinet, he retrieved a large brown paper bag, snapped it open, and moved to the shop floor.

Some soup would be a nice variation. He perused the selection. Beef and barley seemed appealing. He placed three cans in the bag. Corn on the cob, two rolls from the newly opened package of paper towel, eggs, bacon, cream for his coffee, a green apple, two loaves of bread, and six chocolate bars were added. He stood for a moment and thought. What else? He returned to the display cabinet and opened the rear sliding panel. Eddie helped himself to four packs of du Mauriers, placed them in the overstuffed bag under his arm. He switched the inside lock button on the wooden door to locked, pushed open the jangly screen door, and closed the wooden door behind him. He depressed the thumb plate and pushed on the inside door. Locked good and tight. The jangly bell screen door slapped shut behind him as he strolled across to Merv's.

Back beneath the car in the garage bay, Merv missed Eddie's approach. Eddie quietly lifted his items into the back seat of the Rolls and strode to the bay. Merv was scarcely out from under the car before Eddie had retrieved cash from his pocket and handed it over with his thanks.

Eddie hastily retreated to the Rolls and pulled away. The road home was blissfully quiet. Not a car or human in sight. Smoke from a du Maurier trailed in the wind behind as the Rolls ferried him down the road. Even overcast weather couldn't diminish the beauty of this place. The darkening clouds overhead segued into sound. Mozart's Requiem came to him, and Eddie hummed along as he drove.

Travis Smith was Rhonda's one and only child. Over the decade or so they'd known one another, Eddie had tried to offer helpful suggestions to Travis when their paths crossed. Eddie would have placed him somewhere between thirty-seven and forty. In fact, Travis was twenty-eight. He'd been an unwanted late-life surprise for Rhonda at the tail end of her second marriage. Rhonda had never had much interest in Travis, preferring instead to spend her leisure time circling words in word search booklets. It was not, however, Rhonda's neglect that precipitated Travis's impulse toward self-annihilation. It was husband number three, who Rhonda had met shortly after fleeing husband number two, when Travis was no more than six months old. Ted Lumley was a machinist living in the south end of Hamilton when Rhonda arrived from North Bay.

Ted was by all accounts an excellent machinist. He was also a sadist with a penchant for torturing children. Among his repertoire of predations, Ted enjoyed extinguishing his cigarettes on Travis's back. He liked to choke Travis into unconsciousness, drip lemon juice into his eyes, scrub his anus with coarse sandpaper, twist his arms behind his back, and a lengthy list of other macabre, medieval punishments for imagined infractions. After fourteen years of marriage, and only when Ted turned his violent inclinations toward Rhonda, did she make a run for it—with Travis as unwanted baggage.

At the time, Rhonda had neither seen nor heard from Travis's father, Daniel Smith, in fifteen years. She'd fled that matrimonial home with a black eye, fat lip, and bloody nose. As far as Rhonda knew, Mr. Smith moved on to his next target and married her seven or eight years after Rhonda left. As these things go, Daniel Smith died within weeks of her departure from Mr. Lumley. At loose ends and without work, Rhonda's luck quickly changed. Evidently, Mr. Smith had a life insurance policy through his pulp and paper mill employer that entitled the beneficiary to a modest but not inconsequential amount of money. When Mr. Smith remarried, he'd forgotten to remove Rhonda's name from his insurance policy and name his new spouse as beneficiary. Similarly, his son Travis was the named beneficiary of the commuted value of a small employment pension.

It didn't trouble Rhonda in the least that her former husband's most recent spouse survived on a disability pension, and that the woman had been left next to nothing. Within weeks Rhonda had purchased the Mercantile and a small plot of land outside of Cailly. As his legal guardian, Rhonda had taken Travis's pension inheritance and purchased two small second-hand trailer homes for the lot. There, Rhonda left the teenage Travis mostly to his own devices, each occupying their own trailer.

The wind was high when Eddie made his final descent from the bush trail to the cabin. Whitecaps lined the lake, and the faint scent of autumn was in the trees. Cooler weather was coming. He took his cut log from the edge of the firepit and headed for the dock. There he sat atop his log, taking it all in. As the whitecaps ruffled the lake and the wind blew his stringy grey hair, Eddie lit a cigarette and wondered at the beauty of this pristine wilderness. The lake and trees in high wind brought the drama of Wagner to mind. Eddie smoked his cigarette and watched the waves swell as the "Ride of the Valkyries" played in his head. Soon enough it was time for a drink.

Eddie headed in and poured himself a long single malt. He flopped himself into his recliner and took the mail from his pocket. Placing his drink on the floor beside him, he flipped through the envelopes. A charter air carrier looking for money, a nearby country club looking for payment on several pricey dinners, and an envelope postal stamped in Sagaponack, New York. Sagaponack could only be one person. He knew what was coming.

Annabel Novak-Gordan
3 Montauk Gardens
Sagaponack, NY
11962

Dear Edward,   Aug. 23, 2022

    I spoke with Nathan last week. He called about your most recent disaster. I can only say it's a blessing Mom and Dad aren't alive to witness any of it. I haven't seen it myself, but Nathan said the Globe and Mail did a front-page story featuring pictures of decades of your debauchery. Disbarred!! Bankrupt!! Really, Edward? For the life of me, I cannot understand why you remain utterly unable to stay out of trouble. It was humiliating having to listen to Nathan drone on about you.

    Well, I guess all of your high flying and high rhetoric have met their final end. Nathan said the article talked about how you swindled a lady into giving you her RRIF money, an expensive diamond ring, and her condo in Florida—or something to that effect. He said the article talked about how her grandkids won't get any of her things and the woman's son is out hundreds of thousands of dollars because of you. Honestly, Edward, stealing from children? You really have no shame.

    For years I defended you to Nathan and Debbie (and Aunt Elena when she was alive). When Nathan called and told me about all of this, I was in a corner and had nothing to say in your defence. I'm sick of it, Edward. I'm just sick of all of it. The women, the gambling, the drinking. This is why you weren't invited to Christine and David's wedding. You absolutely cannot be trusted. I'm sorry to say it because I know the pain it causes you, but Denise's sister was right to take Melanie. Really, Edward, it's a good thing she's nowhere near any of this. Can you imagine?

    We've come to a point where I now feel it necessary to clarify certain things. I have spoken to legal counsel here and been advised to tell you; in so far as you do not pay rent, you are not a tenant and have no right of *occupancy. You live at the cabin at my pleasure until I say otherwise. Dad did very well to keep your name off title. I'm sure he could have predicted this very eventuality. To lose the lake in a bankruptcy would have destroyed him.*

You've always carried on as though the place were yours. It's not yours. My name is on title for a reason. I've never complained about how you use the place, never asked you to do anything there, never once expected to be welcomed there. At no time have I ever even asked you for the property taxes. (Which have gone up $280.00 in the last four years.) You have enjoyed the lake and occupied the cabin for free, and because of it, my lawyer advises me I can now expect various parties to come snooping around. The thought of Canada Revenue Agency, creditors, bankruptcy investigators, etc. pulling title searches on the property has me very on edge. And so, I'm letting you know in the nicest way possible, unless we can find some alternative, I am considering selling the cabin and the land. To be perfectly clear, I have no interest in profiting from such a sale, and I am only proposing it because Christine and David have no interest in the place.

Yes, I do realize this is not the ideal way to transmit this information. Believe me, Edward, I have no desire to be writing handwritten letters on this or any other subject. It's absurdly Victorian. Despite having repeatedly asked before, I will ask yet again; will you please get a phone and internet? This is not the most efficient way to conduct business.

I'd like to speak with you on the phone about the cabin. I'm not going to revisit any of our previous conversations about your lifestyle and behaviour. That's hardly useful at this point. Please be in touch sooner rather than later. You have my number.

Best regards,

Annabel
PS Christine and David send their love. (Jeremy just graduated primary school!)

Eddie sat for a moment, gathering his thoughts and drinking his Scotch. This was a twist he hadn't seen coming. To have so consistently skated through life inventing ways to avoid accountability, responsibility, or comeuppance, and in the end to be undone by his own sister. It was beyond anything he could have imagined. Edward R. Novak had spent his entire adult life ducking and dodging the Law Society, landlords, creditors, women, and all manner of thugs and ruffians. He'd made an art of it. Now faced with the unfathomable possibility of losing the one thing he could not stand to lose, he found himself in an unfamiliar world. This scolding was different than any of Annabel's previous harangues. He couldn't quite put his finger on why.

Despite the impulse to fire off a blistering response to his backstabbing sister's treachery, Eddie understood the need for a calm and reasoned response. He'd undertake that task when he'd thought through his position. Eddie didn't lack savvy in managing others. Governing himself, however, was another matter. Eddie's hedonistic self-indulgence was tempered only by threats to his essential comfort. Annabel's timidity in the face of even the slightest scrutiny or adversity was pathetic. Why couldn't she just firmly dismiss any inquiries about ownership, beneficial or otherwise? The property was in her name. How difficult would it be to summarily dismiss and deny any inquiry intended to establish Eddie as the beneficial owner?

Eddie lit a cigarette and topped up his drink. The scenario proposed in her letter was potentially catastrophic, but as he reasoned through it, Eddie saw the cracks in Annabel's position. She hadn't said that she was *going* to sell; she'd said she was *considering* selling. She hadn't said it was a binary, sale–no sale proposition; she'd floated the idea and used the word *alternative*. And on the subject of finding an alternative, she hadn't used the word *I*; she'd used the word *we*. In effect, she might have been soliciting Eddie to resolve the matter for her or at the very least, remained open to his input. Still, the very notion of his sister squeezing him off the property greatly rankled him. Notwithstanding his sister's weak-kneed anxiety, when he examined the fact pattern more closely, he found his anger directed as much at himself. It had been a strategic error on his part not to have manoeuvred his sister away from nominal ownership at an earlier moment.

Eddie sipped his drink as a pittering rain began. All this business would require consideration and thoughtful planning. Bach Sonata no. 2 in A Minor was the appropriate complement for this particular rain. Eddie retrieved his tape player and basket from the porch shelf. He pushed the Play button and reseated himself. He began to consider the indignity of his possible removal from his spiritual centre. The place he felt most at rest. The place his soul resonated in perfect pitch.

He thought of the many indignities he'd endured. The disappointments. Why had the press turned on him so mercilessly? Why, when they had so celebrated his arrival, did they so gleefully chronicle his missteps? Why had the Law Society been so painstaking in their examination of his personal conduct? Why had his creditors been so heavy handed? Why had Judith been so mean spirited in her refusal to take him back? Why had his former law partners declined invitations to speak on his behalf, not once, but repeatedly?

Eddie allowed himself this momentary lapse into resentment. But he'd been alive long enough to know this was a useless indulgence. For now, he must think and plan. Rain, single malt, and Sonata no. 2 were the perfect antidote to these tribulations. Annabel's impulse in the face of unwanted scrutiny would require deft handling, creativity and finesse. These characteristics were his strong suit. Had he not time and again fallen from the sun, licked his wounds, made conciliatory noises at just the right moment, reingratiated himself, charmed, seduced, and risen? Resilience was his life's work.

The sound of wind in the trees grew to a steady roar amidst now pelting rain. Eddie pondered all of these things, sipping his single malt and drifting into a blissful wasteland before retiring to bed. Night descended, the tempest blew, rain fell, and sleep came. The hours passed, and Eddie drifted in dreams. Visions of his younger self, at twenty-three, his stealth in the wild. Placing his feet so gently, so silently on the earth beneath him. The scent of prey in thick forest, in cold November air. His ears attuned to the faint alert of a rustling branch, a snapping twig. His eyes narrowing beneath a pine bough. Raising his rifle and taking an eight-point buck from forty metres. He skinned and field dressed the buck on his own. He made repeated trips in and out of the bush to retrieve the quartered meat. Eddie fed seven families that autumn.

In the early morning hours, Eddie awoke to the sound of far-off thunder. He drained the dregs of liquor from his glass, stepped out into the cool dampness, trundled to the edge of the forest behind the cabin, and dribbled out his swollen bladder. He scanned the skies and walked to the dock. The lake was calm this morning. Perfect for an exploration. At the sandy shoreline beside his dock, he flipped his overturned canoe onto its hull. He took his paddle from inside the canoe and pushed the vessel into the lake, hopping in before his feet touched water.

Digging deep with his paddle, he slid along the shoreline to greet whatever creatures he might discover. A mink, an otter, frogs certainly. He paddled the full south end of the lake, rounding north past the granite cliffs, finally resting at the mouth of the driftwood bay across the lake from his cabin. There he sat, enjoying his morning smoke, looking at his shoreline, his cabin, and the high horizon of trees behind it. What a wonder his life had been here. More than seventy years of heaven on earth. He thought of his childhood years, building tree forts and sandcastles, swimming, wandering the bush, gathering wild blueberries. He thought of his teen years: smoking marijuana, reading southern gothic literature, competing at the regatta. He thought of his adult life, fishing, making love to Judith on the ground beneath a stand of maples. Making love to Denise against a poplar tree, and of course that bittersweet morning when he was informed of her death while he played with Melanie.

As Eddie surveyed the sky above the grey horizon, a shattering noise rang out. A rumbling explosion followed by a plume of fire and smoke rising high above the tree line in the direction of Cailly. Masses of scattering detritus fell from the plume. He could tell from the distance behind the tree line, it was many kilometres off. Eddie turned the canoe to the middle stretch of lake and began to paddle straight across in the direction of his cabin. It was an eight-minute paddle on still water. The opening horns of Mahler, Symphony no. 5, rang in his ears as he dug in. The music was short lived. Eddie wasn't halfway home before the sound of sirens in the distance came.

Chapter 4

Eddie wasted no time, pushing himself as fast as his legs would carry him up and down the heights and dips of the trail through the bush. He was keenly aware that the markers of civilized settlement—roads, buildings, a post office—were nothing more than a comforting illusion here. This was wilderness with only the most basic amenities. A flood, a lightning strike, a fire, a rock slide, downed trees, all of these things threatened those amenities. These were community events that required labour. The highlands were not a place to rely on public service personnel. Fact of the matter was, public service personnel were few and far between, and poorly equipped. Disasters, natural or otherwise, required the participation of community, and the community was small.

Merv would know what was happening. Eddie raced the Rolls up the quiet main drag. Merv stepped through the bay door as Eddie pulled in. Face blackened, covered head to toe in soot, carrying five shovels, two pitchforks, and a hoe in his arms, he hot-footed straight to the Rolls, piled the gear into the back, then took the passenger seat. "Go," he instructed.

"Where?" Eddie asked.

"Rhonda's. Go, go, go."

Eddie wheeled the car around with quick efficiency and sped up the street west across the river bridge toward the big highway. Rhonda's residence was four minutes west on the county road and two minutes north on the concession. As they rounded the S-bend just outside Cailly, Jeff's pickup appeared in the distance ahead.

"Travis blew his place up," Merv advised.

"Dead?" Eddie asked.

"Me and Darren looked. Nothing." A foreboding rose up in Eddie, quickly followed by a resolute girding. The two sped close behind Jeff, turning up the concession. Bits of wood, metal, insulation, and plastic littered the road a full kilometre off. The chemical stench of burnt plastic filled his nose; smoke billowed up above the trees. Quiet calm settled on them as they pulled into the blackened dirt driveway and onto the lot behind Jeff. The scene of carnage caught Eddie off. Stepping from the Rolls, he took it all in slowly. A giant field of charred ruin. Left of the driveway, forty metres up, flaming piles of debris circled the crumpled, twisted, black metal frame of Travis's former trailer home. Further into the burnt trees up a single lane extending past the ruins, Rhonda's trailer sat covered in detritus, blackened with smoke and ash. Rhonda rested silently on the bench of an ashy picnic table.

A fire engine and wilderness rescue truck were parked amidst the ruins with their oscillating red lights flaring against the blackness. Lofty pines surrounding the explosion site shot flames high into the air. Five, maybe six other pines further into the surrounding forest were catching fire. Eddie moved quickly to the twisted metal ruins.

"No, Eddie," called Merv. "We tried. It's too hot."

"Where's Murray?" Eddie asked.

"Gone to get Dougie's flatbed. We need the Bobcat. He's gonna get the flatbed and pick up the Bobcat from my place," said Merv before marching off, shovel and pitchfork in hand.

"Where's Darren?" Eddie called after him.

"Gone with Murray," Merv hollered back.

Jeff came direct from his truck to Eddie.

"Get me an axe and a chainsaw, Jeffrey."

Nice but very dim, Jeff Mitchell followed instructions well, racing off to the back of his truck.

Eddie moved swiftly to firefighter Brian Dowd who was removing equipment from the rescue truck. "Brian, where are the rest of the boys?" he asked.

"Just me and Jamie right now. Pete's off with a knee thing. Danny's on holidays. We called over to Sprucedale and Huntsville to get guys to come up, but none of them could come. They wouldn't have coverage if they came. Called down to Lake of Bays and asked those guys to come. They said they'd come, but they'd be two, maybe three hours anyway," Brian explained.

"We need to put the trees out," Eddie said.

"We've only got the one pumper."

"I'm going to take them down," said Eddie, pointing to the flaming trees.

"All right," Brian said.

"I'm gonna drop them right into the centre of this pile. Keep them away from the trees behind."

"You can't," said Brian. "There could be bodies under the wreckage. You'll have to drop them in the bare strip between the piles of debris and the edge of the bush."

"I'll drop them exactly where you want them."

"I'm gonna put you in a fire jacket and a mask, Eddie. Tell the others to put masks on. There's ammonia here," said Brian.

And drop the flaming trees, he did. Precisely where they needed to go. Moving methodically from tree to tree, Eddie chopped and sawed as they rained down burning branches and flaming embers on top of him. Firefighter Jamie followed Eddie around, dousing the fallen trees. Brian and Merv used rakes and shovels, hoes, and pitchforks to look for bodies but found nothing. Darren and Murray arrived and quickly joined Jeff in moving sand onto the flaming debris. Fires continued to pop up throughout the piles of detritus for hours.

Three hours in, Rhonda brought the men sandwiches and water. Eddie sat with her for a few minutes in the interval while he ate. Keenly aware that her son was missing, he was careful in his words. He didn't want to give false hope, nor did he want to discourage. The seven men laboured for many hours before replacement firefighters and rescue personnel arrived from Lake of Bays. Eventually, the police came and determined it to be a crime scene. A major traffic collision had occurred on the far side of the police detachment's territory. It had taken all three of the detachment's cruisers and personnel off the road for hours. Eddie had a quiet word with the police detachment commander before leaving.

Cailly and surrounding region were abuzz for days after the explosion. All sorts of stories and theories were bandied about. Everything from barbecuing accident to intentional bombing. Travis hid out for a few weeks at a friend's boathouse an hour away in Gravenhurst. The police eventually found him hitching rides on Highway 11. He'd left his meth lab in a scrambled mess the morning of the explosion. Bottles of drain cleaner, jugs of antifreeze, old batteries, blister packs of cold remedies, and lantern fuel had been left strewn throughout the interior of his trailer. He'd gone down to the river bridge to do business. When the explosion rocked the area, he'd known what it was immediately and grabbed the first ride he could find out of town.

Despite the fact that no human remains were discovered on the lot, Christopher "Viper" Davies remained missing. There were certainly those who assumed he'd been incinerated on-site. And then there were those who just thought all the attention and heat on Travis had encouraged Viper to relocate. Either way, he hadn't been seen in weeks. Travis, out on bail, was now skulking around town like some sort of Boo Radley character. He was facing considerable legal jeopardy in the form of criminal charges. Specifically, Production of a Controlled Substance, Mischief Endangering Life, Arson by Negligence, Criminal Negligence, and Possession for the Purpose of Trafficking. These were serious charges. Not the easily dismissed, simple possession charges of his carefree teen years.

Eddie had his own challenges. He'd taken his time in considering his sister's anxiety about being the nominal owner of the property he occupied. Eddie settled on the idea that whether her perception of him was fair or unfair, it didn't matter. At the end of the day, his sister wanted no part of him. She wanted to completely disassociate herself from him. He understood this. The task at hand was to facilitate the disentangling. Edward R. Novak had ideas on the subject. They would take time though. For now, he'd write to her. He wouldn't provoke her in any way or give her reason to act precipitously.

This was a matter of some delicacy. On the one hand, it was in his interest to maintain the status quo. The property remained in her name; she paid the property tax and never darkened the door with her presence. This had worked beautifully for Eddie for many years. On the other hand, Annabel was given to fits of pique. She could be bloody vindictive if she felt wronged, and perhaps more importantly, she wasn't fond of Eddie. He could live with her scorn, but the property going to someone outside his immediate family? Never.

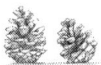

Eddie woke to an early September chill as mist rose from the water at the break of morning light. He paddled across the lake and sat watching his little cabin in the woods as he finished his morning smoke. The view was spectacular. Perfect for contemplating the right approach with his sister. The serenity and solitude of the lake provided the focus required to work through exactly the right tone and message he was looking to deliver. The written word, however, was not Edward R. Novak's strong suit. It was his delivery and theatrical flair that won him accolades. How he drew a jury in with his skeptical and impish questioning, meticulous summaries, argumentation that ascended from plodding dismantling to pounding denunciation. Then a dramatic drop to intimate beseeching.

Eddie Novak was an orator, not a writer. He delivered arguments with such elan and stealth that, by the end, he could make a jury feel as though they were in league with him to right some grave injustice. He could make them hunger to acquit. But Annabel was not a jury. His oration would have no effect on her. In fact, it might do more harm than good. Annabel had had a front-row seat to the Eddie Novak extravaganza for seventy-seven years. She'd seen his act, and it had worn thin decades earlier. He would not risk a conversation with his sister. Despite her request for a phone call, the safest path was a letter.

With a blueprint in mind, Eddie carried on around the north end of the lake. He took his time paddling the shoreline. The outline of his approach was there. The minute details were what required polishing. The peril he faced was existential. There was no room for error in this endeavour. Precision was essential. But not just precision of intent. What was needed here was prose that disarmed rather than alerted. Prose that would buy him time. The essence and energetic vibration of each and every word would need to be scrutinized.

Eddie knew the stakes. He considered very carefully every angle and every possible outcome, or at least the ones he could anticipate. Among the angles to consider was the audience his letter would likely reach. Certainly, Annabel would show it to her husband, Chip Gordan, and no doubt her lawyer, whoever he or she might be. Eddie began to contemplate his arguments and how they would be perceived first and foremost by Annabel's husband, who would likely wield the greatest influence over her, and second, how his position might be viewed by another lawyer.

Robert "Chip" Gordan had been discharged out of the service at the end of the Korean War. Eddie correctly assumed that Chip didn't like him. In their one and only meeting, Chip had regaled Eddie with tales of the drunken pranks he and his colleagues at Stanford University School of Engineering had engaged in. Failing to see the humour in the assembly and installation of a Sherman tank on the lawn of Stanford's inner quadrangle, Eddie had made his disinterest painfully clear. Eddie despised engineers, routinely telling anyone and everyone that he'd never met an engineer who wasn't possessed of an unshakable certainty that they knew everything there was to know. He loathed their loutish swaggering, their obnoxious and misguided intellectual bullying. Chip Gordan was no exception to his general impressions. Eddie would need to craft text in a way that would not expose himself to further revulsion from his brother-in-law. He'd need to do it in a way that protected him from any admission of error, and too, any implied commitment or contract with his sister.

Eddie beached his canoe beside the dock, flipped it over, and retreated to his cabin. He retrieved his yellow legal pad and an antique fountain pen inscribed with someone else's name from his battered briefcase, poured himself a drink, and assumed his place in the recliner.

Annabel Novak-Gordan September 8, 2022
3 Montauk Gardens
Sagaponack, NY
11962

Dear Annabel,

Thank you so much for your letter. I really treasured receiving it. I am so sorry not to have responded sooner. It's been a very busy time here with some tragic recent community events. You might recall a lady I've mentioned in the past, Rhonda, from the Mercantile. Her son has found himself in a spot of trouble with an explosion at their residence. Attending the aftermath of that scene was quite harrowing. And of course, there's some legal fallout for the unfortunate young man.

Merv from the Texaco asks about you from time to time. If I was a suspicious sort, I'd think he might be sweet on you. Haha. You always were a beauty, Annabel. Still are, I'm sure. I wonder if Christine got your striking features. It's been absolutely ages since I've seen her. I wish you'd send pictures of her and David and Jeremy.

Annabel, I did want to signal my appreciation for your forthright expression of concern regarding the complication of your name being on title to the property. Naturally, you're correct and justified in your concern. You know, as I age, (77, can you believe it?!) I've come to discover that really anything we possess is not truly ours. We are merely placeholders for those that will come after us. The cabin is and has been a lifelong privilege bequeathed from our father. What a visionary he was. I guess we've had the good fortune to be caretakers and stewards of his vision. As great a privilege as it has been, it has also been a responsibility. One that I take very seriously. Knowing how close you and Dad were, I'm sure you see the importance of continuing his memory and legacy.

Your letter conveyed that you're open to alternatives other than a public sale of the property. What a thoughtful and prudent position. Thank you for that. Perhaps I'm overreaching here, but I see your core goodness in wanting to investigate best possible outcomes for the property. Outcomes that allow for continuity of Dad's vision. In that regard, Annabel, I will endeavour to ensure to the best of my ability that your wishes are honoured. Let me do some work on this and get back to you.

I know that you've experienced great disappointment with regard to certain things in my past. I want to assure you that the circumstances described by Nathan are not nearly as one-sided as it would seem. As dear a cousin as he is, Nathan does have a rather florid way with language that, while entertaining, titillating even, is not always accurate.

Though I have not read the Globe and Mail article, I assume it didn't mention that I had a very close personal relationship with the deceased person, who made no secret of her fondness for me. I would also note my dear friend's offspring had been longstanding and noticeable absences in her life, and by their absences, had exposed themselves to reduced participation in her estate. But this is not the moment for relitigation of ancient history.

As for my inadvertent insolvency, my circumstances are not really much different than any of the other tens of thousands of people who've suffered grave and unforeseeable investment reversals. Such is life.

Anyway, enough of that. All of this to say, let's put our heads together and see what we can come up with to keep Dad's memory alive and the property protected from malign actors who may have devious motives. I look forward to being in touch with you on this subject. As the responsible occupant-caretaker, I think it's important that we be on the same page in terms of transitioning title interest in the property. I sensed from your letter that you're committed to thoughtful and methodical management of that process. I'm deeply grateful to you for that, Annabel.

Annabel, will you please do me the great honour of passing along the $50.00 included herein to your wonderful grandson? Please tell Jeremy, his Great-uncle Eddie is immensely proud of him. Graduating primary school is epic.

Much love, Annabel,

Eddie
(P.S I know what you're thinking. 50 Canadian dollars ain't that much in US greenbacks! Haha. Very true.)

Eddie thought good and hard about what he'd written. Was it sufficiently businesslike in its approach to the issue of title ownership? Did it have the desired feel and verisimilitude of warmth and sincerity? Or at least what he thought warmth and sincerity might feel like. Had he been too defensive in his comments about the newspaper article? Did he include statements he might come to regret? Eddie read and reread the letter several times before committing to its contents. He'd done his best, and so he resolved to be content with it. He placed a fifty-dollar bill in the centre of the flat yellow paper, folded the letter over the money, and neatly tucked the pages into an envelope.

Eddie ate a tart green apple and poured himself another drink. He sat a few minutes on the porch and pawed through his basket of cassettes. It was hard to say what he was in the mood for. When nothing caught his fancy, silence suited him. Back in the cottage, retrieving his yellow legal pad, he resumed his place on the recliner and took the fountain pen from the floor by his seat. The time had come. Eddie summoned his courage and began to write a new letter. The most important letter of his life.

Chapter 5

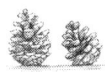

"I've got a couple pieces of mail here that need to go out," said Eddie, detecting a hint of lavender talcum powder in the air.

"I'll take 'em," said Rhonda.

Eddie thanked her, handing over his envelopes, then making his way to exit the Mercantile.

"You're a lawyer, eh?" Rhonda barked.

Eddie turned. "I beg your pardon?"

"You still a lawyer?" she asked again.

"That's a complicated question."

"Huh?" Rhonda grunted.

"I did practise law, yes. Though I haven't for quite some time," said Eddie. "May I ask why you're inquiring?"

Rhonda searched some pages she seemed to be clutching with a measure of anxiety. "What's a pre-trial conference?" she asked.

"Can I assume this pertains to Travis's legal matter?" Eddie asked.

"Yeah. He's got charges. Needs to go to this thing for the trial. Like before it happens," said Rhonda. "What's it for?"

"A pre-trial conference is a meeting of the Crown and defence counsel with a pre-trial judge, who will review details of the case to determine how the trial will proceed and whether some things can be settled before trial," Eddie explained.

"What's this for?" she asked, pushing several pieces of paper in Eddie's direction.

"I assume it's the Pre-Trial Conference Form."

"The government lawyer there, she said Travis needs to fill it out and give it back to the court or something."

"Well, I guess that's what Travis should do then," said Eddie.

"Can you look at it?" asked Rhonda.

"Rhonda, I'd really rather Travis retain practising defence counsel. I think that would be best for him."

"He talked to the one lawyer there down in Collingwood. The man wanted $5000.00."

"That sounds about right," Eddie replied.

"The government lawyer said Travis needs to put this form in right away. It was supposed to be in weeks ago."

"I guess he'd better do that then. Nice to speak with you, Rhonda. Please say hello to Travis for me," said Eddie as he turned for the door.

"Can you help him?" Rhonda asked.

"As I said, I'm no longer practising, and it would be in Travis's best interest to find a competent, licensed legal representative," Eddie advised over his shoulder.

"Just to fill out the form," Rhonda implored. "He didn't do nothin' wrong. They're trying to nail him 'cause of the way he looks." Eddie rested a moment to study Rhonda's face. Her attempt at invoking sympathy was as plausible to Eddie as a seven-year-old's living-room magic show.

"That may well be the case, Rhonda. I don't know," said Eddie. "But as I say, I'm no longer practising, and it's best for Travis to find a good lawyer who can defend him."

"Just to fill out the form is all," Rhonda pleaded. "Travis only got his grade eight. A lot of them words on that form are confusing like."

"Has he spoken with Legal Aid?" asked Eddie.

"The lady there at the Legal Aid said Travis don't qualify. Can she do that?" asked Rhonda.

Eddie deferred an answer as a pair of adolescent girls stepped between his position at the door and Rhonda's roost behind the cash register. The young ladies paid for their licorice and other confection items before leaving.

"I have no idea what's happened in the past with his Legal Aid contacts, so I wouldn't know. I think the thing to do here, Rhonda, is to make some sort of effort to retain legal counsel. That would be best," Eddie advised.

"Can you fill out the form?" asked Rhonda.

Eddie let out an exasperated sigh. Who was he to refuse the downtrodden? With all his might, he'd resisted her imploring, but in the end, he succumbed.

"Look, now isn't really the time for this. You've got customers in and out. If you'd like to bring Travis here this evening after closing, I could walk him through the form, but he'll fill it in himself," said Eddie.

"Okay, how be you come for seven?" asked Rhonda.

"Yes, I suppose," Eddie reluctantly agreed. Glancing up as he closed the jangly bell screen door behind him, Eddie noticed the newly installed light fixture above the shelves in the centre of the shop. He ambled back to the Rolls. Now what was he to do? It was shortly after four, leaving him just under three hours to fill. No sense in making the trip home only to shortly turn around and return.

Eddie sat behind the steering wheel, contemplating what to do. A trip into the liquor outlet and some chit-chat with Darren would kill some time. Then maybe a few minutes with Merv. Eddie pulled the Rolls into the road and took his time to the liquor outlet just down the way.

With the summer crowd mostly gone, the outlet was hardly a beehive of activity. A few browsers slowly perusing was all. Eddie went straight to his regular shelf, retrieved two bottles, and made his way to Darren at the cash aisle.

"Hey, Eddie, how're you doin' today?" Darren asked, running Eddie's bottles across the scanner.

"No complaints," Eddie replied. "Still this side of the soil."

"Let me know when you're lookin' for a hand with the dock," said Darren, who four years running had assisted Eddie with the autumn removal of his dock from the lake.

"Yes, thank you for reminding me. Let's get on that, shall we? Sooner rather than later, but whenever you're available," said Eddie.

"I'm here Tuesday to Saturday. Could do Sunday or Monday," said Darren, bagging Eddie's bottles.

"All right, let's say Monday then."

"Perfect," replied Darren. I'll be out around eleven if that works."

"Sure," Eddie confirmed before asking, "any sign of Viper?"

"Oh, Eddie, you know these guys. He's long gone. Don't think we'll see him around here again."

"You never know," said Eddie, skeptical.

"I don't think so. One of the little meth-heads down in Bracebridge told Rhonda, Viper was down in Kentucky. She was askin' all over about him, worried he was scorched up in a pile on her friggin' driveway," Darren said.

Eddie made way for a customer approaching behind him. "I'm off. I'll see you Monday. We'll have a drink."

Darren bid him goodbye, and Eddie wasn't eight steps out the door when he spied Stephen Coutts marching officiously up the sidewalk toward him. Eddie was not in the mood for Stephen's customary drivel this particular afternoon. Failing utterly to read Eddie's glowering countenance, Councillor Coutts greeted Eddie with aching cheerfulness.

"Good afternoon, Mr. Novak. Lovely to see you."

Disarmed and only slightly perplexed, Eddie momentarily restrained his instinct toward evisceration. "Hello, Steve." He kept moving purposefully to the Rolls-Royce Corniche.

Again, failing to apprehend Eddie's unspoken disinterest in engagement, smiling Councillor Coutts continued. "Stephen, actually. I guess everyone in town's talkin' about how you took those flaming trees down at Rhonda's with the burning branches and that. Good on you, Eddie."

"Not exactly a Herculean task," Eddie demurred.

"You got 'er done. 'Course, takin' trees down in that situation's a little different than just clearin' 'em off," Stephen commented with poorly practised nonchalance. Eddie instantaneously sussed the meaning of all this conviviality. In Eddie Novak's world, villagers like Stephen Coutts were strictly amateurs when it came to mischief-making.

"You don't have enough brains to be an idiot's helper. You're a fucking rube, Steve." Without further ado, Eddie went about his exit from the liquor outlet parking lot, keenly aware that the councillor was up to no good.

Merv was just closing up as Eddie pulled in. "Gas?" asked Merv.

"Just a visit, Mervin."

"Pull round the back," Merv said in invitation.

Eddie steered the Rolls across the patch of dirt around to the back of the creaking stuccoed building. The river through town ran twenty metres behind Merv's shop down to Cailly Lake. Eddie parked in the shade of ash trees and high scrub brush that lined the riverbank. He lowered the top of the Rolls and took in the fresh September air. He pushed the driver's seat back as far as it would go and raised his legs over the door, resting his feet on the side-view mirror. Soon, Merv joined with a pair of dirty plastic cups and what appeared to be a bottle of embarrassingly low-quality blended whisky. Piling himself into the passenger seat and extending his feet over the door onto the passenger-side mirror, he offered over one of the plastic cups and a pour from his bottle.

"Ah, thank you, but no, Merv. You're a gentleman. I couldn't possibly diminish your bottle. I've taken the liberty of bringing my own. I hope you won't mind," said Eddie, accepting the grimy cup.

"Fair 'nuff, Ed," said Merv, pouring from his own bottle. Eddie reached to his feet and retrieved a bottle of single malt, pouring generously into his own cup. There the two sat in the glow of a lovely late summer evening, feet extended over doors, seats reclined, sipping their awful and fine whisky.

"Looks like Travis has really put himself in it this time," said Eddie.

Merv sipped his drink. "That wasn't hard to see comin'."

"His mother says he doesn't have two nickels to rub together to pay for a lawyer. I told him three years ago, cooking was gonna get him into trouble," Eddie exclaimed.

"Trouble? He's lucky he didn't kill himself. Or someone else."

"Rhonda was on me about doing up his paperwork," said Eddie.

"Don't mix in, Ed."

"I already committed. Heading over there later. I'll walk him through the form and then let it go. It's nothing to me."

The river burbled along as the gentlemen rested a moment in quiet repose. Merv slid his fingers round the corner of his jaw and rubbed his beard stubble.

"You watch that fella. I'm tellin' ya, don't turn your back on him, Ed. He's not right."

"That may be the understatement of the century," said Eddie. "Right or not, he's entitled to the best defence he can find."

"Be careful with those people," Merv concluded.

Eddie began to ponder the mechanics of it all. He'd never given much thought to whatever underworld Travis or his mother operated within. His own demimonde was enough to navigate. How was it that after several years of cooking, Travis was unable to lay hands on $5,000.00? A paltry sum in that industry. The trouble and effort to cook wasn't worth it to produce for one's own consumption. Certainly, it helped, but there was no question, cooking meant selling. And selling meant profit. Eddie had seen oddballs in and out of the Mercantile from time to time. And now that he thought of it, he'd heard locals express concern about increased traffic on Rhonda's concession road. Where was the money?

"Missed you at the regatta this year," said Merv.

"Oh, bullshit. You did not," Eddie laughed.

"No, we didn't," agreed Merv.

"I heard Melinda was up to all her old tricks. What did she pull this year?" asked Eddie.

Merv grinned. "Darren or Jeff or someone said she weighted the front of her canoe with a rock for the ladies' single canoe race. Oh shit, I laughed when I heard that."

"That's clever." Eddie took another swig of his single malt.

"She's not stupid," Merv concurred.

"Not bad to look at either," said Eddie.

As the gentlemen laughed and drank, the sun sank below the trees along the river's edge. After a time, a figure appeared in the rear-view mirror behind them. A voice called out.

"What in the holy hell are you degenerates up to?"

Merv and Eddie turned in unison to see Darren making his way across the hard-packed dirt behind the garage.

"Get over here!" Merv hollered.

Darren must have heard them from the street and come to investigate.

"Come 'ere," shouted Eddie.

"I've found the weekly meeting of Cailly High Society," said Darren.

"Grab a cup," Merv instructed.

Darren diverted through the rear door of the garage and returned with a filthy measuring cup.

"Making a recipe?" Eddie asked.

"Hit me with a pour," Darren implored Merv as he took his place in the back seat of the Rolls.

"Hey, kid, this week can you help me get some tires down from the loft?" Merv asked. He'd grown too unsteady to be hauling heavy items down a makeshift ladder. Over the last several years, he'd begun to rely on Darren and some of the other young men in town to help, just like Eddie.

"Sure, yeah. I'll see you Tuesday likely," said Darren.

"You'll have to haul us into the Seniors' Centre soon enough," said Eddie.

"Once I get your dock out and Merv's tires down, I'm puttin' you both on the list. Gonna take you in when you start to nod off in the liquor aisle, Eddie. You'll like it there with Edna and Gladys," Darren joked.

The three carried on drinking, laughing, and fraternizing. An hour or so passed, and Eddie began to survey the passing cars around the corner of the building. He was due soon enough to meet with Rhonda and Travis. A few more minutes of laughing and scratching and Eddie prepared to take his leave.

"All right, gentlemen, must run. You're welcome to continue this little soiree. Mervin, I'd like to borrow your phone briefly if you'd permit. I've got to make a short call to an old friend before I head across the street."

"Sure enough. You know where it is," said Mervin.

"Thank you, sir," said Eddie, tossing the keys to Merv. "Put the top back up when you're done. Leave the key on the seat."

Eddie ducked into the shop through the rear door and made his call before heading out through the front door to Rhonda's. He was four or five steps across the dirt before the sway grabbed him. He steadied himself and took a deep breath in, as though somehow a deep breath through the nose would remedy the effects of half a bottle of Scotch whisky. Eddie wobbled and weaved his way across the road to the Mercantile. Pushing through the jangly bell screen door, Eddie greeted Rhonda and Travis with unusually moist enthusiasm. "G'day, dear friends!"

Rhonda sat on her perch at the cash register, while Travis stood leaning on the customer side of the cabinet. The form papers sat on the cabinet top beside a plastic plate stacked with sandwiches.

"Made some sandwiches, if you're hungry," Rhonda said.

"Ah, how nice. Look at you. That's very sweet. I'm famished actually," said Eddie, grabbing and stuffing half of a ham and cheese sandwich into his mouth.

"What were you gonna say to Mr. Novak, Travis?" asked Rhonda in an alarmingly infantile voice.

Pale and shifting, Travis stammered out rehearsed lines of

apology followed by thanks. "I'm sorry for throwing pickles at you. Thank you for coming and helping me with the papers."

"Water under the bridge," Eddie assured him. "Well, look then, what have we here?" Eddie said, retrieving the papers from the cabinet top.

"Travis says he don't understand none of it," Rhonda advised.

"Oh, is that right? Well, how about we let Travis speak for himself, shall we?" Eddie instructed as he stood perusing the pre-trial form. "What do you have to say about all this, Travis? Get me a pen, would you, please, Rhonda."

Taking a blue pen from the shelf behind her, Rhonda pushed it across the cabinet to Eddie. Wobbling slightly as he turned to face Travis, Eddie wiped away a dribble of mustard creeping down the corner of his mouth.

"Nuthin'," mumbled Travis.

"Your trailer blew up on its own, did it?" asked Eddie.

"Yep."

"Right. Okay." Eddie went about the business of flipping through the twenty-six-page pre-trial form. Placing the form on the cabinet top, he began checking boxes. Within a few minutes, the form was mostly complete.

"Who's the prosecutor?" Eddie asked.

"Karen somebody, I think," said Travis.

"The Mulgrave woman," Rhonda added.

"Karen Mulgrave?" Eddie said, grimly.

"That's her," Rhonda confirmed.

"Step over here, young man," Eddie said. "Print your name here at the top, then sign back here on the last page."

Quickly complying, Travis printed and signed as instructed.

"Tell me, what other paperwork have you received from Crown counsel?" Eddie asked.

"Nuthin'," said Travis, making no effort to conceal the aggressive scratching of his pubic area.

"Nothing? You didn't receive any disclosure documents from the Crown?"

"What's disclosure?" asked Travis.

"Never mind. Suffice to say, you didn't get any other paperwork, correct?"

"No."

Eddie emitted a loud burp. "Excuse me. Now around the time of the explosion, you were where?" Eddie asked.

"Gravenhurst, no, I went to Gravenhurst after," said Travis.

"All right, so, where were you when the explosion occurred?" Eddie asked.

"Under the river bridge," Travis disclosed.

"All right, under the river bridge. And were you with anyone at the time?"

"Viper."

"Christopher Davies, is that right?"

"I dunno. I just call him Viper."

"Okay, so, at the time the explosion occurred, you were with Christopher Davies under the river bridge, but then went to Gravenhurst?" Eddie asked.

"Yeah."

"Be sure to tell whoever represents you all of these things. Tell your defence counsel that you were never provided with copies of the police file, investigating officers' notes, or the forensic report."

"He don't have no lawyer, Eddie. Should he ask for all that?" Rhonda asked.

"Yes. Right away," Eddie explained. "He'll need to give it to whoever he finds to represent him."

"Can you talk to them for me?" asked Travis.

"Talk to them? Travis you're in it up to your neck, son. These are penitentiary charges if they stick. You need a lawyer. This is not a joke. I talked to you about the cooking, long ago."

"Travis, go down to the cellar and get the root beer from the shelf beside the freezer," Rhonda ordered. In that moment, Eddie saw in Travis the unmistakable look of fear. A look he knew well. Travis sighed and shuffled off to the back, through the hall, and down the stairs. Rhonda quickly skirted round and took a place in front of the cabinet beside a now unsteady Eddie. Positioning herself close by his side, Rhonda began examining the paperwork on the cabinet top. "What're all these papers for? What does it mean?" asked Rhonda, as the two stood side by side facing the looming dread of judicial administration.

"It's agreements and admissions from both the Crown and the accused. A judge is going to review this and meet with the Crown and Travis's counsel. The judge will sort through what the issues are, who'll testify, what they'll testify to, and so forth," explained Eddie.

"Travis can't go to jail. He can't do no time, Mr. Novak. I don't know what I'll do without him," Rhonda whimpered. Though in full glow and teetering, Eddie wasn't so far gone as to be incapable of appropriate skepticism.

"Rhonda, Travis needs a lawyer. This should have been the first order of business the day he was charged."

"They want so much money. Travis don't have $5000.00."

"Really? Is that right? Tell him to get a loan from his business partner under the bridge," Eddie slurred. The words barely fallen from his lips, Eddie felt something curious below his suit jacket. Rhonda seemed to be scrutinizing the pre-trial form as her right hand drifted over and came to rest on Eddie's penis.

Eddie smiled, let his head fall back, and thrust his hips slightly forward, pinning Rhonda's hand between the cabinet and the front of his pants.

"We can help each other," said Rhonda.

"Mmm. Right. Look, your boy is in some serious, serious trouble," Eddie moaned.

"Can you talk to the government lawyer? Travis don't have no money," Rhonda whispered.

Eddie saw Rhonda anew. He gave her scrutiny in a way he never had. Her grey and brown shoulder-length locks, the over-tanned, dimpled skin of her decolletage, the post-menopausal rolls of flesh beneath her mauve, polyester blouse. Her flattish bottom. The curve of her drooping, pendulous breasts. Her sad and wanton weather-beaten face with its clumpy mascara, blue eyeliner, and slightly rouged cheeks. "When is the pre-trial conference?" he asked.

"Next Friday, one thirty," Rhonda answered, gently cupping his privates.

Eddie turned to face her and reached for her left breast. Lifting and squeezing, he spread his fingers to feel the fullness of it, exploring her nipple with his thumb as she measured the length and girth of him with her palm. "Tell Travis he needs to go to the court office tomorrow and give the clerk the form. While he's there, he should find the Crown counsel office and ask for the disclosure documents. They'll give him a package. Tell him he needs to give the package to Darren. Darren's going to bring the package to me on Monday. I'll look at it. Travis needs to leave town on Wednesday. He needs to disappear and not return until after the pre-trial. Make sure no one sees him leave. Send him somewhere no one knows him. Tell him not to say a word to the clerk or the Crown or anyone else about any of it," Eddie instructed. The sound of Travis's footsteps cued Rhonda to return to her perch behind the cabinet.

"There's no root beer on the shelf. I looked everywhere," Travis complained.

"I'll look myself," said Rhonda.

"I've given your mother some instructions, Travis. She's going to walk you through what's going to happen. Do just what she says, all right?"

"You gonna talk to them for me? Please, Eddie. Can you please talk to them for me?" a now twitching Travis implored.

"Just do what you're told, Travis. I'm going to come and sit with your mother at her trailer on Wednesday evening, and we'll go over some things. Eddie turned to exit and bid them adieu. "I'll see you Wednesday night, Rhonda." And out the jangly bell screen door he went, staggering his way back to the Rolls-Royce Corniche.

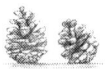

Eddie awoke to the faint chirping of song sparrows in the ash trees by the river. With the emptied bottle still cradled in his arm, he arose from a crumpled heap on the back seat of the Rolls. Stepping out, he stretched and yawned, walked to the river's edge, stepped into the brush, and after a lengthy wait, relieved himself. Despite the cool predawn air, Eddie lowered the top of the Rolls. He lit a cigarette and pulled out of Merv's back parking area. The drive back to the cabin at sunrise was glorious. He hummed the entirety of Scene 1. from Pyotr Tchaikovsky's, *Swan Lake*.

After stowing the Rolls, locking the shed, and hiding the key, remaining bottle in hand, Eddie readied himself for the hike along the trail. He made his way to the opening in the brush where the trail began. There in the dirt, he noted the unmistakable wheel tracings of an all-terrain vehicle. Tire tracks made Eddie uneasy. He didn't like people snooping around the property for any reason. He wondered as he walked. There was no cause to think it might have been hunters. Hunting season didn't open for weeks, and besides, all the locals knew the trail was the entry point of the Novak property. Any hunting would require permission.

Whatever angst Eddie might have felt quickly lifted. Sunrise in the heart of the wilderness was too magical for such discomfort. The scent of pine and earth too intoxicating. As he made his way through the thick forest along the dirt path with its rocks and roots, he contemplated the coming week: the intimacy and certainly the relief he'd experience. Rhonda had made her interest clear. Eddie took it as self-evident that, at sixty-eight years old and single, Rhonda would naturally have needs that were not being met. He'd always considered himself a reasonably attractive man. Not conventionally handsome per se, but still, he was tall, had decent teeth, hair on his head, and remained as agile as a man half his age. Why wouldn't she make herself available to him?

All of this seemed a more pleasing narrative than the alternative. Eddie supposed it could be faintly possible that Rhonda might be under the impression that he remained a licensed legal practitioner. Sure, perhaps she might think he was qualified to assist her son, but really, the thing he'd come to conclude was that women enjoyed him and found him sexually attractive. As Eddie crested the top of a hill halfway home, deep in the thickness of woods, a sound caught his notice. A low bugling he knew all too well. Stopping to get his bearings and searching for cover, Eddie stepped quietly off the path into the brush. He pushed himself a few metres into the underbrush and rested on his haunches.

Eddie waited as the bugling continued. Not more than a minute passed before he heard the crashing and snapping of saplings and brush thirty metres further up the path. The sound drew near, and Eddie sat motionless. The ground began to vibrate beneath his feet as the thundering drew close. Then, from beneath the cover of a blue spruce, he saw what he knew was coming. Eddie watched as a bull moose near eight feet high pushed its way down the trail past his place in the bush. He watched as the animal laid waste to saplings, scrub brush, and small trees caught in its enormous rack. He rested in awe of the sheer size and majesty of it.

After the passing, Eddie emerged slowly from his spot in the undergrowth, his bottle still in hand and unscathed. He was no stranger to moose encounters and knew well to keep away from a bull moose in rut. An adult bull was capable of grievous bodily harm and was not to be provoked or engaged. Eddie listened carefully to the sound of the bull moving away. He waited for the sound of other moose further up. It was not entirely unlikely that the moose was being run off by another larger, more aggressive male. One that might be more deadly than the one he'd just avoided.

Moving forward with all due caution, Eddie remained on alert. He marvelled at his good luck to have been so close to one of the great beasts of the northern wild. Taking great pains to remain quiet as he stepped and careful not to rustle the encroaching brush, Eddie moved with agility and stealth over the bumps and divots in the trail. He was not two hundred metres down the path before his senses began to tingle. The hair on the back of his neck and forearms stood on end. A deep knowing stopped his feet. He felt the wind at his back and quickly removed his grubby suit jacket. He took his wallet from the inside pocket and threw the jacket as far as he could into the line of scrub to his left. Dodging quickly into the forest to his right, he jostled his way around trees and undergrowth, forcing his way deeper into the bush. Then in an instant, he heard what he'd sensed. He froze midflight as a shiver ran through him.

The menacing yips and growls of a pack pierced the solemn Algonquin morning. Eddie sought and found a large oak and stepped out of view behind it. He waited in silence as the pack descended the trail above him. Wolves on the hunt were not to be interfered with. A single wolf might not stand a chance against a bull moose, but half a dozen would certainly bring an end to even the largest moose. Eddie knew their lethality. The rising sun dappled light through the canopy onto the ground as he stood contemplating the possibilities. Wrapping his palm around the cap of his tightly clutched bottle, he twisted the cap, tilted the bottle to his mouth, poured as much as his mouth would hold, and swallowed. Then he waited in the ominous noise of hungry animals.

The barking and growling slowly faded as the stalking pack continued their pursuit down the trail. Eddie was not impatient to resume his trek. The possibility of a straggler wolf was not beyond his imagination. He sat for many minutes, resting his back against the oak. He wondered just then, who, if anyone, would look for him if he was taken by the wolves? The opening notes of "O Fortuna" filled his head. Drama was not what he'd expected this morning. After a long swig, Eddie rose and returned to the trail. He surveyed the clutter left by the moose and breathed deeply to catch the scent of any other wolves. He retrieved his coat from the woods on the other side of the trail. His chest hot from liquor and rising sun, Eddie continued his way home.

No small relief filled him as he ambled down the gentle slope to the cabin. He stopped momentarily to enjoy the glinting sun on the lake. Eggs, toast, and a swim were called for. A flash of white caught his eye as he rounded the side of the cabin to the steps and doorway. There he found a sheet of paper taped to his door. What might this be about? Stepping up the three wooden steps, he ripped the paper from the door and began to read.

Township of Perry
1695 Emsdale Rd.
PO Box 70
Emsdale, ON
P0A 1J0

SORRY WE MISSED YOU!

Dear Occupant,

A site visit was conducted concerning a bylaw or zoning agreement matter. Please contact us at your earliest convenience. When contacting the Township Office, please make reference to your lot and plan number.

Thank you.

Matt Monwil
CBO and Bylaw Official

Hi Eddie, come by the office when you can. Thanks!
Matt.
Sept. 8/22

Eddie smiled and shook his head. The little shit, Councillor Stephen Coutts, was having some fun with him. He walked to his cooking pit, took a cigarette and lighter from his pants pocket, lit the form letter on fire, and started his cigarette from the flame. He tossed the flaming page into the pit and placed some kindling twigs on top.

Eggs and toast from an open grill were always a satisfying feed. A faint buzz from morning liquor made his breakfast that much sweeter. Eddie nibbled the last bits of egg-soaked toast, took his skillet and fork to the lake, and scrubbed them clean. He stripped himself naked and plunged into the lake from the dock. Despite his years, Eddie could still dive with decent form. The lake was cooler this morning. The warm surface water of midsummer had begun its turnover to the lower depths. Night-cooled water now sat atop. Eddie didn't mind. The bracing water made him shiver and reminded him he was alive. He swam to the middle of the lake and rolled onto his back to enjoy the cloudless sky.

Bobbing and drifting, Eddie sensed a faint vibration in his chest that rose quickly and overcame him. It was a minute before he recognized it. He was no aficionado of opera, but he knew Catalani. *La Wally*, Act 1, filled his ears. Floating naked beneath the sun and sky, ever so briefly, Eddie touched the divine.

As the music in his head dissipated to the heavens, Eddie rolled onto his stomach and began the front crawl to land. He steadied his feet in the sandy bottom approaching the shoreline. Ankle-deep, he turned to face the lake and took it all in for a moment. The land, the lake, the trees, the sky; they would hold long after he was gone. He found joy in that knowing, thankful for the gift of his life. Cold, cold water streamed from his body as he strode out of the lake onto the land. Standing ashore, Eddie shook his limbs, noting the disappearance of his penis beneath his protruding stomach. Hoisting his belly up, Eddie marvelled at the tight retraction of his testicles. A momentary reprieve from the usual tripping hazard, he thought.

Chapter 6

Melanie Novak's long legs required the full length of stirrup leathers. Taller than most women, atop a horse near eighteen hands high, she was an imposing figure. Blade was the largest mustang anyone at the Bureau of Land Management had ever seen. The wrangler gentleman from the bureau was quite enthusiastic about him when she called to inquire about adopting. She'd heard from a colleague in the English Department at Casper College that the bureau was in possession of several superb new captures. She'd seen him from her truck when she pulled into the parking lot. The connection was instant. Melanie broke and trained Blade herself. His teeth seemed to suggest he might have been four or five years old when she took him. He was trailered and brought back to the ranch immediately after they met.

Melanie watched a west wind ripple the grasslands of the western plain from eight hundred yards above on a high plateau. She'd cut trails from the rear acreage of the ranch through scrubland and up the side of Casper Mountain. As they traversed property boundaries on their plodding ascent, neighbours often welcomed her and Blade. Melanie was careful to remain on excellent terms with her neighbours. She knew well that a few cross words could jeopardize her pathway up the mountain. But the Garlands were a quiet, unassuming old Wyoming family, and there wasn't a local in the county that would have denied a Garland passage across their land. Melanie used an access point to public trails that led to the plateau, a hundred yards from the mountain summit. She routinely rode Blade to the plateau and sat overlooking the magnificence of the western plain and endless sky.

Melanie organized her life around two foundational pillars: her teaching schedule and her riding habits. She'd been around the college long enough to understand that having good relationships meant greater control over her class schedule. Slowly but surely, her reputation for gentleness and warmth had won her friends in the right places. After several years, calls from Professor Novak's office to the scheduling office were being returned. It was no longer a problem to have an 8:30 a.m. class shifted to 10:00 a.m. or to move a late afternoon class in the dead of winter to an hour earlier. With just the right schedule, Melanie could do a short ride in the morning and be home after classes for a longer ride before the sun set.

Angela Garland was not by any means a warm person. From the earliest days, it had been made clear to Melanie that Angela was her aunt and not her mother. Melanie was ten years old before it began to strike her as unusual that, despite being routinely reminded that Angela was not her mother, her actual mother, Denise, was rarely if ever spoken of. There were pictures she'd seen over the years in old scrapbooks, but it was clear, questions and discussion about her mother were not welcome. Or at least, not comfortable territory with her aunt, Angela; and grandmother, Theresa. She couldn't recall a single occasion when her father's existence had been acknowledged or his name spoken.

Theresa passed in the late 1990s when Melanie was a teenager. Melanie had good memories of her. Theresa had been a nurturing and loving grandmother, and her death was an unmooring of sorts for Melanie. Despite best efforts at warmth, Angela was never quite convincing. She'd never wanted to be a parent. Denise's shocking death had been traumatizing for Angela, the sudden responsibility of raising a child, an anchor she could never have anticipated. Her life changed overnight. Any affection she might have felt toward Melanie had always been tinged with a mild seasoning of irritation.

Brought to the ranch directly from Toronto weeks shy of her second birthday, Melanie joined the generations of Garlands who had watched the changing seasons from the base of the mountain for over a hundred years. The ranch, comfortable but far from the ostentatious display they were more than capable of, was her great-grandfather's original homestead. Aside from Angela, Melanie was the only other remaining descendant of the first Garland on the mountain and was now the caretaker.

After more than thirty-eight years on the ranch together, Melanie took Angela to an assisted living facility in Casper. Angela began showing signs of cognitive impairment at the relatively young age of sixty-four. Over a year or two, she became unusually reclusive, preferring to stay in her bedroom rather than walk the ranch as she had for decades. In her final six months with Melanie, she'd become aggressive and combative. This was a drastic departure from her ordinarily austere and calm demeanour. Melanie made the final decision when Natrona County Search and Rescue had to be called. Angela had gone missing in the middle of a June night. She'd wandered off and was found four miles on foot from the ranch.

Melanie never married. She had the misfortune of adverse

events in early adulthood that made her both weary, and wary of men. For decades, the Garlands of Wyoming had been stalwarts among the Church of Jesus Christ of Latter-Day Saints. Before his early death, her grandfather had been deeply involved at the ward and stake levels as a bishop and president, and eventually a regional seventy. Her aunt and grandmother, with whom she'd lived exclusively, insisted she attend Brigham Young University across state lines in Utah. Melanie went for her freshman year and was miserable. Her only interest in leaving Casper was to gain exposure to young men, to whom she'd had little access. Life on a relatively isolated ranch with two older women had not been ideal in this regard.

On arriving in Provo, Melanie was initially impressed with the homespun charm and handsome features of some of the young Mormon men. She was not, however, enthused about their reticence and awkwardness in the area of intimacy. By that point, the dictates and tenets of the Church were of little interest to her. With her interests and needs unserved, Melanie convinced Angela and Theresa to allow her to transfer to the University of Chicago, where she did her undergrad in English literature. She followed with a master's degree in cultural anthropology at the University of Nebraska and a PhD in American literary studies at the University of New Mexico.

To her aunt, Melanie's education seemed an impossibly impractical life path. Garlands were people of the land. The esoteric and arcane concerns of academia were at best, silly, at worst, not to be trusted. Melanie tried in vain to explain to her aunt the meaning of her PhD thesis, "Gender Expression in American Prairie Literature and the Writing of Willa Cather."

Melanie took work teaching at a college in Cheyenne for two years before returning to Casper. She'd intended to stay on, but

Angela had pressured her to return. By then Angela was alone on the property and found the solitude not entirely to her liking. When Melanie finally agreed to return, Angela made phone calls and arranged an interview for Melanie at Casper College. However stoic her aunt had been, she was never unhelpful. Though Melanie routinely visited Angela in the assisted living home, it seemed to Melanie that Angela wasn't always sure who she was. To help, Melanie repeatedly referred to her as "Aunt Angela."

After Angela's relocation, Melanie had plenty of time for academic research, paper writing, grading student work, listening to music, and riding. Blade had been a good friend to her for many years. There was a rapport there. They knew one another's moods and were respectful. Riding up and down the mountain trails, across the expanses of plain, a bond had formed. Blade was Melanie's only true companion. Certainly, she had work colleagues with whom she occasionally socialized, but Professor Melanie Novak was not one to habitually mix and mingle.

After Angela's relocation, Melanie wondered how she might manage the property on her own. Whatever concerns she had quickly eased. Of course, there was plenty of work to do, feeding and grooming Blade, household repairs, fence maintenance, mowing, and so forth. But Melanie Novak was nothing if not capable. She had skills for life on the ranch. It was all she'd ever known. Watching her grandfather, her grandmother, her aunt, and extended family pitching in, managing the land, the building, and the barn, Melanie had absorbed the rhythm and demands of the place. She'd learned how to work and developed a network of locals to call for jobs she wasn't fit to do herself.

As the sun began to set, Melanie clucked and tugged to let Blade know it was time to go. The pair slow-stepped down the mountain trails back to the ranch barn. Blade had been unusually well behaved today, not obstinate or difficult responding to direction. When she stabled him, she poured a long drizzle of molasses into his feed. She troughed his evening haylage, freshened his water, said her goodnight, and strolled back to the house under an orange-pink sky.

A shower, a quick bite to eat, an hour or so of reading in her chair, and Melanie was ready for sleep. Her nighttime routine was usually a hasty affair. Teeth brushing, lights out, and straight to bed. She didn't enjoy this part of her day. Nor did she enjoy meals by herself, often preferring to eat from containers, standing in the open door of the refrigerator. Not by any means spinsterly, Melanie had had love affairs with several men over her life. Some more important than others. But the long drought of inactivity she'd been experiencing in her romantic life was beginning to wear on her. The few single men she encountered at work were dull and badly dressed academics for whom she felt only pity and embarrassment.

Melanie lay awake. What was she doing here? Of course, she loved Blade, the family homestead, and teaching, and Wyoming. She had lovely friends. Smart and decent people. But what was it about this moment that left her feeling so adrift? Her grandmother and aunt had certainly been good to her. They'd had their flaws, naturally, but Melanie had had a good upbringing. Her grandfather left them comfortable and never in need. And yet, there was something she couldn't quite discern. What was it? Being alone was not the worst thing. Her solitude had enabled her to research and write extensively. Indeed, she'd published more academic papers than any of her colleagues.

Melanie contemplated the balance of her life. She was pleased with her situation in academia. It suited her. She'd always been scholarly, loved English literature, and enjoyed sharing her knowledge with bright young students. And yet here she lay, hungry for something she couldn't quite assemble in her mind. Pondering the nature of this malaise from the comfort of her bed, Melanie laughed quietly, envisioning herself as a sort of western Emily Dickinson character, squirrelled away on a ranch. The image of it amused her.

Night fell. Melanie sank into deep restfulness. Sleep came. The hours passed. Under cover of darkness, images surfaced. Cool amber light, a muscled stallion strode, black, glistening; a white mare sparkled in the mist. The steam of their warm bodies rose over the plain. They advanced toward the light of the eastern sky, a roan yearling striding between. Mare cast a watchful eye. Stallion led. Protected. Tails flicked. The yearling followed. Stallion's thick, wide haunches gleamed. Mare whinnied, shepherding yearling. Sun crested mountain tops, flooding the western Great Plains. Stallion and mare become vapour. The yearling trailed, wandering alone. Stirring followed. Melanie awoke to fresh light. She lingered in the quiet of her warm bed.

Melanie knew these horses. Many nights she'd caught their scent, seen their vague silhouette, felt their warmth, lingered in their afterglow, floating in the timeless place of rest and wakefulness. But as always, the comfort of their presence was punctured. Melanie had to lecture today. "*Sarah, Plain and Tall*: Love Story or Commodification of Womanhood?" Were her notes ready? Would other faculty attend? Melanie hauled herself from bed and began her day.

The drive to the college was no different than any other day. Parking, as uninteresting as ever. Melanie's lecture was more anticipated by students and faculty than her. There was little doubt in anyone's mind, Professor Novak was among the most compelling university English literature lecturers in the western United

States. Melanie Novak had made a name for herself with her lectures. Bringing prose to life for young minds with insight and colour. She was unparalleled by any of her peers. She delivered flawlessly. Thoughtful questions received compelling answers. Pleasant chit-chat enlivened the reception following. It went quite as expected.

Melanie resisted the instinct to dissect the response to her lecture as she went about her errands. Groceries, banking, and a final stop at the veterinary office to pay for last month's field visit. A persistent case of mud fever required the veterinarian to treat Blade. Upon arrival at the ranch, there wasn't sufficient light left for a ride. Melanie had to content herself with feeding and watering Blade before leading him on a short walk around the paddock. Any time alone with her companion was time well spent. Blade disagreed. The sun drew down quickly, and she tried to coax him back to his stall. He wasn't budging. Melanie wrapped her arms around his enormous neck. "Please, Blade. I'm tired." Blade snickered. She rubbed his side and took a small apple from her pocket. The treat taken, Blade conceded in a slow march to his stall.

Amidst the straw bedding, Melanie placed her head against his massive neck, and Blade lowered his head and rested it on her shoulder. The tightness in her chest released, and a sob erupted. Tears flowed. She clung to his mane as he rubbed her face with his head. Melanie cried without shame or restraint. The tears and sobs continued unabated, escaping through the barn doors into the still Wyoming night as she held him to her. Finally, Blade shifted his weight with impatience. Melanie's clutching, the sobs, the tears, disconcerting to him. With a final rub of her face, Blade lifted his head and nipped her shoulder. "Ow!" Melanie laughed and patted his neck. "Brat."

Melanie lay awake in her bed well past midnight, listening to the sound of crickets chirruping through her open window. She'd done well today. Faculty were impressed, and students made wiser. Melanie gathered herself, lifted her head from the pillow, turned on her bedside lamp, placed her feet on the floor, and pulled an envelope from the drawer of her night table. She took yellow legal paper from the opened envelope and began to read, yet again, a letter she'd read many times since its arrival.

Melanie Novak September 8, 2022
17 Hogadon Rd.
Casper, WY
82601

Dear Melanie,

    It's not clear to me if you are still at this address. It was the address listed on the postcard I have kept on my nightstand for quite some time. And I had a vague recollection of the address from many years earlier when your mother and I were together. Since the end of my legal practice, I no longer have a phone or access to the internet and now rely on the ancient art of letter writing. In any case, I very much hope this letter reaches you and that you and your Aunt Angela are both well.

    I realize how impossibly presumptuous it could seem that you would welcome any contact from me. I send this correspondence with the full knowledge that it may offend. I'm aware that best wishes at this point may be adding insult to the injury of my absence from your life. That said, I find myself with no other means of establishing contact other than a simple letter and the ordinary salutations one expects.

    In the interest of brevity, I will come straight to the point. I reside on land in mid-Northern Ontario. This land was transferred to your Aunt Annabel by your grandfather, and she has generously allowed my occupancy for many, many years. For reasons I won't go into, my sister has recently expressed a desire to have her name removed from title to the property. To that end, I wanted to make you aware of these developments and to solicit your interest in becoming owner of the property.

I'm sure all of this is very unexpected; however, it bears reminding, with no disrespect to your proud Garland heritage, you also have a Novak ancestry. An ancestry that includes generational possession of a remote piece of property with a large swath of untouched boreal forest, a pristine lake, and a comfortable little cabin.

The property is yours if you decide to accept it. In the event that you did accept ownership, I want you to know, I would bear any cost of maintenance, upkeep, and property taxes. The awkwardness of this is extremely disquieting, however . . . At the risk of being a major imposition, should you accept, I hope that you would allow me to continue living on the property until such time as I am deceased. Not that it's of particular concern to you, but I do feel the need to be transparent; I would be completely at peace dying on the property as I have no interest in being housed in an assisted living or long-term care facility. If you want to accept the property as your inheritance but feel no inclination to allow me to stay, I would completely understand and would make other arrangements. Indeed, it might be a well-deserved fate. I'm sorry to be so morbid, but these are the considerations one thinks about at 77 years of age.

Melanie, apart from details about inheritance of the property, the true intent of my correspondence is to shamelessly request that you come to Cailly and see the property and lake. I am well aware that I have no business making such a request. That aside, I hope that you will consider coming.

Without other options and against my better judgment about mailing cash, I've included $3000.00 in this envelope for travel expenses. If you choose not to come, I accept this. In that case, please spend the money in whatever way you wish.

And now for the most awkward part. How do I sign off this

missive? "Dad" seems inappropriate. "Father" seems unnecessarily sterile. What a conundrum.

Best wishes, Melanie,

Eddie
PO Box 71
Lot #84, Fire Route 9
Perry Township, Ontario
P3A 1J0

PS Annabel told me several years ago, you're a Professor of English literature. I'm very proud of you.

Chapter 7

Eddie rested a moment against a ragged birch tree at the end of his sandy little cove. He caught his breath while Darren jiggered the dock onto a flatter position on the grassy sand. Heaving and hauling the dock out of the water had become increasingly difficult for Eddie. He hadn't been able to manage it on his own for several years, but the two had done it again, pulling the dock from its position on a stone crib and laying it up on shore safe from winter ice. One more item addressed and taken care of. Any further swimming would be started from the shore.

"You're a good man, Darren. Appreciate the help. Guess I owe you a drink," said Eddie.

"You guess? Shit, you owe me the bottle. That sonofabitch is heavy," Darren chided.

"Kid, I'm telling you, getting old is the pits. Can barely get my ass out of bed and it's fifteen minutes to take a leak." Eddie rubbed his back gingerly.

"Right. Thanks for that. No kidding though, Eddie—if there's other stuff you need done, just come let me know, and we'll do it together," offered Darren.

"Careful, now. I may well take you up on that," said Eddie.

"I'm serious, Eddie," said Darren. "Don't try getting up on the roof or any other foolishness. I can come whenever you like."

"Message received, with thanks," said Eddie placing his hand on Darren's shoulder. "Those drinks won't pour themselves, young fella. The single malt is calling." The men retreated to the cabin.

Darren McIntyre meant it when he offered help. He and his wife, Beth, were small-town lovely. Throughout the afternoon, the drinks flowed, and Eddie tortured Darren with his cassette tapes of classical favourites. They laughed at the disparity of their tastes, neither bothering to convince the other of anything. As the day wore on, bawdy jokes, loose and lively conversation ensued. Eddie delighted in the camaraderie. He missed his old life of revelry. It was nice to have a friend there. Someone to drink with and laugh. Darren was a convivial and willing accomplice. His innate intelligence and curiosity pleased Eddie. Darren peppered him with questions about his most entertaining and intriguing trials, hanging on Eddie's every word and prompting him from one story to the next. After a half a dozen drinks, there were few who could rival Eddie as a raconteur.

Life in Cailly made for curious alliances. The small cluster of humans in a vast and rugged terrain had its own social order. Generational differences meant little. Fewer people meant fewer options for companionship. As entertained as Darren was with Eddie, Eddie found safety in Darren's workaday sincerity. Other than the pleasure of Eddie's company, Darren wanted nothing from him.

After much lubricated thanks and commitments to reconnect and share a glass, Darren left to meet up with Beth. Alone now, Eddie began preparing for an evening of work. Dvorak's Serenade for Strings was the appropriate selection for the tedium of picking through the Crown's disclosure documents. Placing himself comfortably in his recliner, drink and yellow legal pad at the ready, Eddie tore into the folder of police reports, summaries, their scant notes of the scene, poorly taken photos of the destruction, 9-1-1 transcripts. He scanned and read each document once over to absorb its general sense of purpose or thrust. A second, closer reading yielded thoughts, observations, evaluations as to the relative quality and merit of each item. And then, on third reading, Edward R. Novak, pen in hand, began the demolition of the case against Mr. Travis Smith.

Eddie made short work of most of it, furiously scribbling notes that would wither even the most convincing Crown witness. Even deep in his cups, Edward R. Novak was better than most. A lifetime at trial had honed within him a masterful eye for spotting weakness. He looked at officers' notes, the descriptive language used, sentence structure, presumptions, subtle inferences, the chronology of events, errors of fact. The Crown certainly had foundational grounds for suspicion. A trailer in the woods doesn't simply explode for no reason. Such an event does not, however, at least in Eddie Novak's world, constitute a criminal proceeding. Travis's case was the first legal file he'd looked at in the two years since his suspension and eventual disbarment. The feeling was bittersweet. To the extent he was not being paid, not in the traditional sense anyway, he was more of an informal helper rather than a legal agent.

Among the many reasons Eddie was a pariah among certain lawyers was his vindictiveness in defeat and indecorousness in victory. He'd never been a gracious winner. He made a point of rubbing his victories in the noses of opposing counsel and prosecutors, and he'd never once shaken hands with a prosecutor or joined one for a friendly drink after a trial. Eddie lacked collegiality. He loathed prosecutors and made it abundantly clear. Indeed, Edward R. Novak had gained infamy in Toronto for his gloating and snarky remarks to opposing counsel in hallways and elevators. There was no lack of clarity about Eddie's primary instincts. Atticus Finch, he was not. Eddie cared little for fair administration of justice. He was driven by a bottomless well of contempt for prosecutors.

After several hours, Eddie finished his note-making, retreated to his bed, and lay in deep contemplation. How was it he knew this name, Karen Mulgrave? Who was she? Where and when had he encountered her? It was his habit to know the opposition, their personalities, quirks, foibles, triggers. He'd excelled at flattering egos, admonishing scamps, schooling bullies. It's what his clients were buying. Not to mention that he'd made a career of gaming the system by dodging tough prosecutors and judges with last-minute rescheduling, feigned illnesses, requests for changes of venue, accidentally misinforming opposing counsel, and any number of other antics intended to advantage his clients. In his many years practising, Eddie had mastered the game within the game.

Searching his memory, Eddie recalled one of many pre-trial discussions concerning an alleged Highway Traffic Act charge of his own. Eddie's recall rarely failed him. This was no exception. He had indeed spoken with Ms. Mulgrave once. Not that long ago in fact. About three years earlier. He'd always driven and parked exactly how he pleased without a care in the world for the rules of the road. Speeding violations, driving the wrong way on a one-way street, illegal turns, failure to stop at red lights, all part of Edward R. Novak's ordinary day. After finding her name on the trial schedule for his matter, and after getting a physical description of her from a court clerk, he'd happened upon Ms. Mulgrave in the hall.

Opening by complimenting the young woman's blouse, Eddie had suggested that perhaps his speeding violation had been related to a grievously ill family member who wasn't expected to survive the day, and that conducting his vehicle so recklessly was completely out of character for his ordinarily scrupulous care. The fresh-out-of-school prosecutor had been persuaded to take Eddie at his word and extend generosity to a fellow member of the bar. Charges dropped.

Eddie considered the time that had passed since his last encounter with Ms. Mulgrave. She'd practised now for several years. She was less green. She might be in her early thirties at this point and have eased into that period in any young lawyer's life when they have practised long enough to make the mistake of believing they know more than they do. This would be her weak spot. Ms. Mulgrave's self-concept could undermine the Crown's position and be leveraged to Travis's benefit.

Whatever leverage Eddie believed he might hold, there remained the problem of his advocacy. Eddie was disbarred and, perhaps more importantly, disgraced. An outcast. The greater obstacle to acquittal under the circumstances was not the Crown's evidence but Eddie's inability to access the levers of justice. He wouldn't be permitted to act on Travis's behalf. The Crown or a pre-trial judge even entering into an informal discussion on the subject of Travis Smith's criminal charges was a remote possibility at best. Undaunted, Eddie continued calculating. Edward R. Novak specialized in remote possibilities.

He ran through various scenarios. Under what circumstances might he find a listening ear? What would motivate a prosecutor or pre-trial judge to entertain his commentary? How could he gain entry to the conversation? How could he encourage trust and disarm them? Eddie wasn't unaware of the effect of his reputation and persona. He knew that any appearance of an agenda would result in an immediate termination of discussion. There was strong likelihood that, after Eddie's first encounter with the younger Ms. Mulgrave, she'd have eventually heard of his reputation for chicanery. There would be no extension of generosity or benefit of doubt in his favour this time.

Evidence and obstacles aside, as had always been the case, Eddie was happy to gamble on random chance, fickle winds of fate, and fluke possibilities. In this particular case, it'd cost him nothing, and the reward of relieving tension and having needs met was a reward he'd take. Certainly, intimate relations were sufficient incentive to involve himself here; but the undeniable truth was that he remained constitutionally incapable of resisting the sheer fun of having sport with a prosecutor. A withdrawal of charges or acquittal of Travis Smith was unlikely, but Edward R. Novak had routinely been the beneficiary of prosecutors unwittingly filling holes in his defence by presenting Crown witnesses who inadvertently gave exculpatory testimony. This was his stock-in-trade.

As odious as Eddie's behaviour had been throughout his legal career, no one had ever accused him of the dump-truck practices of other defence counsel who took large retainers, rarely left their offices, and dumped cases in plea agreements. The courtroom was Eddie's office. The stage he strode. But this was not that stage. This was the backroom of the justice system, where Edward R. Novak's theatrics amounted to little. Travis Smith had placed his trust in Eddie's ability to grease the wheels in his favour. In this case, the endeavour would require a great amount of luck, some stealth, and a dollop of something like sincerity. Luck being beyond Eddie's control of course; stealth on the other hand, very much within his command. As for sincerity, Eddie had been faking that since the day he was born.

Morning sun glinting through his dusty window, Eddie lazed about in bed relinquishing dreams and considering the passage of time. It was Tuesday. A relatively meaningless marker in a life without employment. Eddie measured time by seasons now. This Tuesday, however, was unlike most other Tuesdays in Eddie's recent history. This was the day before his visitation with Travis's mother. Eddie would shortly be relieved of a great deal of tension in his mind and body. He lay on his back amidst a sprawl of grubby sheets, the sound of Saint-Saëns's *The Carnival of the Animals* percolating beneath the images in his mind.

Eddie rubbed his eyes and staggered to his feet. It occurred to him in that moment, for the first time, that perhaps his body's capacity for alcohol and recovery therefrom might not be what it used to. His legendary liver might be beginning to falter. Powerful thirst and a slight ache in his head caught his attention. Water was required. Finding a jug of bottled water, Eddie poured himself a tall glass and swallowed as much of it as he could in one go. He removed himself from the cabin and ambled to the edge of the wood behind. Standing naked on dew-dampened ground in the cool morning, he waited. This was not time well spent. Finally, at long last, his bladder released, and he was given relief. He tired of the constriction of his urethra and the frustration of waiting. And too, the occasional dribbling and uncontrolled spurts.

Eddie wasted no further time, moving quickly to the shoreline, wading in, and plunging under. The bracing cold caught his breath and brought him fully alive. A morning swim, coffee, several cigarettes, three plums, and quiet reading filled the hours. One hundred and four pages into *The Book of Negroes*, Eddie placed the tome on the floor beside the recliner and rested his eyes. There in rest the anxieties came. What of wayward Travis?

Could he remain out of sight? And the seemingly determined Karen Mulgrave. How would she play her cards? And Annabel, with her campaign of righteous indignation. What would it take to pacify her? The very notion of a public sale of his lifelong idyll was upsetting. His bankruptcy and disbarment came to mind. Lurking in the shadow too was Stephen Coutts and his childish attempt to prosecute some trifling offence. Memories of his former legal partners and their disdain arose. And of course, doubts concerning Melanie's reception of his letter crept in. Would she agree to become the owner? How would she interpret his request? All these things, these errant strands fusing to a single troubling whole.

Easing to his feet, Eddie lumbered to the shelf by the porch door and laid hands on his bottle and glass. He removed the cap from the bottle and stood in thought. What if he'd blown it? How did one repair damage to a relationship that hardly existed? The fact was, Eddie knew precious little about Melanie. Whatever narrative he had in his head about who she might be could be utterly misguided. And on a balance of probabilities, what little she knew about him was more than likely not good. On what basis would she have any regard for a stranger, much less accept an invitation to the Canadian wilderness from him? Surely the invitation to come to the property had been an overreach. Why? Why was the invitation extended? Eddie had baffled himself. The weight of it was unsettling. Eddie returned the cap to the bottle and placed the glass and bottle back on the shelf.

Retrieving his yellow legal pad and antique fountain pen of suspect provenance, Eddie took to his recliner.

Melanie Novak September 13, 2022
17 Hogadon Rd.
Casper, WY
82601

Dear Melanie,

    I'm sorry to be a bother; however, there was much I left out of my correspondence of 5 days ago. First, I feel the tone of my letter might have seemed quite discordant with the reality of our situation. After sending the letter, it occurred that although you are my daughter, and I am your father, the truth of the matter is, we do not know each other. Receiving a letter from me may have come across as a dissociative act of someone who isn't particularly in touch with reality. My apologies in that regard. So where to begin? Perhaps by introducing myself.
    I was born in the fall of 1945, shortly after your grandfather's return from the war. Your grandfather worked as a mine engineer in the north, which is how he became familiar with the property I now reside on. At the time, land loans were available to former military personnel. Your grandfather acquired the land with the assistance of an advantageous purchase price and low interest rate, available under the Veterans' Land Act.
    Although we lived locally in my early childhood, your grandfather eventually moved from mine sites well north of here to the executive offices in Toronto. I graduated from Malvern Collegiate in Toronto in 1963, obtained a degree in English literature at Western University in London, Ontario, and returned to Toronto to pursue a law degree through Osgoode Hall. I finished my law degree in 1970 and then travelled for 2 years. After stays in Kathmandu, Marrakesh, Ibiza, Bali, and Negril, I returned to Toronto, wrote

the bar exams in 1972, and began practising civil litigation and criminal defence law.

It was often a great pleasure to defend unwarranted criminal charges and correct systemic injustices that deprived my clients of their rights and freedoms. Along the way, I had the good fortune to be a participant in some very pivotal case law that advanced the cause of civil liberties.

My practice of law came to an inglorious end after nearly 50 years. In the many decades I practised, I had the pleasure of defending hardened lifelong criminals who were a significant and ongoing danger to society, marginalized members of society experiencing intermittent encounters with the justice system, casual perpetrators of crimes of opportunity, individuals whose criminal charges overreached beyond actual offences, ordinary folks who made a singular bad choice, and my favourite but rarest of clients, completely innocent people charged with offences they did not commit.

Beyond my law practice, I greatly enjoyed travel and music. Over many years, I travelled to several countries in South America, the Far East, most of Europe, the north of Africa, Eastern Europe, and several places in the Middle East. I always made a habit of seeking out the music and regional cuisine of the countries I visited.

In 1974, I married Judith Hansen. Although I loved Judith dearly, our lifestyles were not compatible. That is to say, she objected to every one of my ignominious habits. In 1978, I met your mother. Amidst ongoing conflict with Judith, I fell, like any sentient male would, for Denise Garland. Your mother had come to Toronto with a former boyfriend 6 or 7 years earlier. From what I can remember, he had been a ranch hand, or something to that effect, somewhere in Wyoming. If I recall correctly, he had received a draft notice from the United States Military and quickly departed for Toronto, with your mother following shortly behind. The gentleman eventually acquiesced to his family's wishes and returned to the United States. It was my impression from many conversations with your mother that she did not feel welcome to return to Wyoming.

    I met your mother at a dinner party held by mutual friends. To say I was taken with her would be an understatement. Your mother was the most impossibly beautiful person. She radiated goodness. It would not be true to characterize my love for your mother as being related in some way to the disintegration of my marriage. The failure of my marriage to Judith was the by-product of my hedonistic and libertine life. I married your mother immediately after my divorce from Judith.

    I hope that you will allow me the indulgence of sharing certain thoughts with you, namely, the ever-present spirit you have been in my life. Your birth was the purest joy I have ever known. I have spent an eternity in the thrall of the memory of you. The months I spent with you and your mother were the happiest days of my life. The look of unfiltered glee on your face when I walked in the door at the end of the day has sustained me. It is no small thing to be the object of a young child's love. Because of you, I have experienced that privilege. Though I cannot know nor do I presume to know your feelings about contact with or from me, I was encouraged to write based on your phone call several years ago and the thoughtful postcard several years before that. Rightly or wrongly, I took these things to mean that you are not entirely averse to communicating with me. I accept whatever feelings you may have.

    I have thought of and wondered about you every day of my life since the day you were born. I have seen you in my mind's eye as a tiny newborn. I have treasured the memory of carrying you on my back in the waters of Cailly Lake. I have seen you as the toddler with whom I played on the floor of your grandfather's cabin. I have imagined you as a youngster joyfully roaming the plains of Wyoming. I have imagined you as a young lady, graduating secondary school. I have envisioned you striding across a stage to accept a college degree. It has been my sincere hope that you have found and known the bliss and comfort of romantic love. I have wanted more than anything to believe that you are well loved by a steadfast partner. But most of all, I want you to know, you were conceived in love. Your mother was the kindest, sweetest, most generous person I have ever known.

It has been brought to my attention by others that it may well have been a blessing that you were not exposed to your father. On the assumption that any child would likely have some degree of curiosity about their parents, it's easy to imagine that you would have questioned family about me or done your own investigation. A simple internet search would yield considerable clarity as to the full extent of my dissolute, profligate, and licentious life. On that subject there's no intent to mitigate or conceal. For the entirety of my life, I have neither been good nor decent in my behaviour.

For what it's worth, my greatest regret is that you have suffered because of the choices I made. Melanie, I have no excuse. I failed you. If it gives any comfort whatsoever, I am truly sorry. I say this with no expectation of forgiveness. And I accept your disinterest or refusal to communicate with me.

In so far as I have been a failure as a parent, the very least I can do is to offer whatever information you may want concerning myself or your Novak family. At your request I will answer any questions, truthfully and to the best of my ability.

On my best day, I was never worthy of your mother's love. I don't doubt that you are the best of her and without my deficit of character. Your Aunt Annabel and cousin, Christine, have from time to time shared with me that you are entirely enchanting in conversation. They have marvelled at your elegant and deft turn of phrase, and too, your abundant graciousness. This has given me great pride. Thank you for your willingness to be in phone contact with your aunt and cousin. News of you has more than once been a lifeline I desperately needed.

I hope that this information gives you a clearer sense of some aspects of who I am beyond what is contained in public records. It should have occurred to me before sending you my last letter, that in effect, you'd be receiving correspondence from a relative stranger. Needless to say, one doesn't immediately welcome such entreaties. I felt it necessary to ease whatever concerns you might have and to broaden the palette of information available to you.

As indicated above, I would be pleased to answer any questions concerning myself, members of the Novak family, our history, or any other aspect of interest to you. The offer is made without any expectation or inference toward commitment or obligation on your part. (That sounds very legalistic. Excuse the terminology. Old habits.)

With the greatest love in my heart,

Eddie.
PO Box 71
Lot #84, Fire Route 9
Perry Township, Ontario
P3A 1J0

CHAPTER 8

Eddie flipped the headlights on as the sun began to dip below the tree line. He rubbed his hand around the smoothness of his clean-shaven face. A quick glance in the rear-view mirror to check his washed and combed hair. The colours of autumn had begun to appear in the trees. Not as spectacular now at dusk but enjoyable nonetheless. Humming Ravel's *Boléro*, Eddie conducted the Rolls around the corners and over the hills of the Almaguin Highlands. Along the way, he considered the extent to which he would share certain information with Rhonda. Expectation management was required. He couldn't expose himself to Rhonda's or Travis's disappointment in the likely event of failure. It would be made clear, any participation on his part was a long shot.

Eddie accelerated the vehicle directly up the driveway to Rhonda's smoke-stained trailer. Rapid departure from a woman's residence being a skill Eddie had honed over a lifetime, he spun the Rolls around and positioned the vehicle for a forward exit. After emerging from the sumptuous Rolls-Royce Corniche with a vague whiff of liquor, cigarettes, and urine about him, Eddie did a quick straighten up of his pants and jacket. He mounted the metal steps to the trailer and knocked. A familiar frisson rose up within him, a sort of primal stirring.

Eddie stepped around the door as it swung out toward him. Rhonda stood in the doorway, resplendent in a well-worn powder-blue velour leisure suit, with matching eyeshadow and rouged cheeks. Long, yellowed toenails curled toward the floor from her bare feet, brassy, nicotine-stained hair cascading over her slumping shoulders. The lowered zipper of her leisure top offered only the slightest hint of bosom. Eddie stepped forward into the drab, faux-wood-panelled trailer.

"Hello, Rhonda."

"Hello, Mr. Novak."

"We have much to discuss," said Eddie.

"Did you read the papers Travis got from them at the courthouse?" Her words coming so quickly on one another as to be almost indecipherable.

"I did."

"What should he do?" Rhonda inquired.

"Where is Travis?" Eddie asked.

"He took the bus to Guelph."

A gentle smile curled the corners of Eddie's mouth. "Guelph? Why Guelph?"

"You said send him where he don't know no one."

"Not exactly. I said he should be sent somewhere no one knows him."

"Why's he gotta be somewhere like that?" asked Rhonda.

"You don't need to know. I was hoping we could sit to discuss this."

"Okay, just clear the junk off that couch there, and we can sit. You wanna drink?"

Eddie moved across the musty lime-green shag carpet to an

orangey floral-print couch pushed against the side wall in a makeshift living area. He removed the tabloid detritus and placed himself on the centre seat. His eye caught a curious gleam of chrome atop Rhonda's sticky kitchen countertop. A rather haute-looking coffee maker, the value of which likely exceeded the value of the trailer itself. Rhonda took a bottle of gin and plastic children's cups from a cupboard with a broken door. She poured gin, took flat tonic from a small fridge, and topped up the cups before placing the drinks on the milk-crate coffee table. Returning to her kitchenette, Rhonda retrieved a lawn chair from its place by the Arborite kitchen table. She returned to the living area and placed her chair opposite Eddie on the other side of the milk crate. "Travis can't do no time. If he pays a fine, can that get him out of it?" Rhonda asked.

"Why don't you come sit over here with me to discuss this?" Eddie said. Eddie's words failing to register, Rhonda continued with her inquiries.

"If you talk to the prosecutor lady, can you ask her to take a fine? Does he have to go in front of the judge for that?"

"We'll get to all of that. For now, why don't you and I get better acquainted," Eddie suggested.

"Mr. Novak, I'm gonna look after you, but I need you to tell me what to do about Travis. You said he could go to jail. Travis never done time like that before. Always probation and fines."

Eddie took his cup of gin, silently leaned back, spread his knees apart, and enjoyed a pleasing sip. The two sat in extended silence. Eddie took a du Maurier from the pack in his coat pocket, lit the cigarette, and enjoyed a long drag. Rhonda picked up her cup and made her way to the far end of the trailer. She opened, then disappeared behind, a plain wooden door. Several minutes passed. Eddie finished his cigarette and butted it out in the overbrimming ashtray on the milk crate.

Straightening his jacket and fixing his shirt collar, Eddie lumbered through the narrow living room to the far end before tapping gently on the flimsy plywood door. No answer came. Gently turning the knob, Eddie nudged the door open. The tiny bedroom was scarcely larger than Eddie's height and width. A narrow bed and a nightstand with a lamp and a full ashtray was all it held. A haze of smoke hung in the air as Rhonda hauled on a cigarette, her naked body splayed out facing the doorway, legs apart, her sagging, colourless breasts resting atop her fulsome gut. A mass of matted, greying pubic hair failed to fully conceal her tired bits. Eddie stood, watching. Cigarette dangling from her lips, Rhonda used her left hand to fondle her breasts, massaging them, teasing her nipples. She placed her right hand between her legs, allowing her fingers to caress and penetrate.

Eddie removed his jacket, tossing it to the floor. Forgoing buttons, he pulled his dress shirt over his head, piling it with his jacket. He removed his shoes and unzipped his pants. Then he kicked his pants from his legs, removed his stinking socks, and pulled his fetid underwear down from his waist. Rhonda surveyed the landscape of his nakedness as he moved to her bed and seated himself at her feet on the tiny single mattress. He took her by the ankles and spread her legs wider. Without dispatch, she butted her cigarette, stretched forward, and took Eddie by the neck, pulling his head down into the openness of her legs. Eddie lingered a moment, seeing and smelling, before tasting.

Rhonda Lumley believed it was better to receive than to give. Or at the very least, receive first when required to give. Such a modus operandi suited Eddie perfectly fine. Relieved of the expectation to sail at full mast right from the harbour gate, Eddie told himself that giving would help in firming his commitment to the job currently at hand.

Eddie's skills evidently pleased and surprised Rhonda, as if she'd long abandoned the hope of recapturing such sensations. Within short order, the shock and tenacity of Eddie's diligence had Rhonda arching, her toes curling until she shook. Her hips firmly in Eddie's grasp, Rhonda brought her hands behind his head and plunged his face deeper into her. Her nether regions began to spasm. Eddie sensed the quivering of her inner place. Emboldened, he sped up his pace. Then, without warning, there emitted from her backside a loud, fleshy flapping noise, followed by the emanation of an acrid, noxious odour. So close was he, the taste of it made him recoil. Eddie staggered to his feet, gagging. Rhonda, buckling and jerking, scrambled to cover herself with sheets. "Mother of God, what the hell?" Eddie hollered.

"Oh my God. I'm so sorry, Mr. Novak. Oh God, I had cabbage rolls at lunch, and I . . ."

"Christ almighty!" Eddie spat.

"I'm so sorry. Oh God. Oh God," Rhonda cried out as the stinging fumes wafted throughout the impossibly small space.

Eddie's eyes watered as he gagged and convulsed. Rhonda panic-lunged, seizing Eddie by his flaccid penis, yanking him to her.

"Owwww!" Eddie screamed.

Dragging herself to the edge of the bed, "No. No. Wait," Rhonda implored, quickly thrusting her mouth around him. Placing his hands on her shoulders, Eddie steadied his feet on the floor. Withered by the paint-peeling stench and death clutch on his most sensitive parts, Eddie wobbled as Rhonda worked away at him. He longed for an open window as the minutes passed. Concentrating with all his strength, he sensed the beginnings of engorgement. Encouraged, Rhonda redoubled her efforts as Eddie held his breath.

Eddie was halfway to the full readiness he longed for when a familiar puckering began beneath. A dread rose up in him. An urgency he'd struggled with. "Wait . . . Wait," he pleaded.

As if wanting more than anything to bring a rapid end to the event, Rhonda tightened her lips around him and forged on, wrapping her hands around his drooping buttocks, pulling him deeper into her mouth. The agony finally overtaking him, Eddie shoved her shoulders back and pulled himself away from her. A short jet of hot urine spurted forth across her face and bedraggled hair.

"Ugh. You pig!" Rhonda screamed.

"Shit!" Eddie shouted.

"That's disgusting!" Rhonda yelled.

"Oh Jesus, I am so . . . I have this . . ." Eddie attempted.

"Fuck off. I don't know what you're into—"

"No, no, no, it's my prostate! It's not what you think. I've never . . . Come here. Please, I'm terribly sorry. Please," Eddie begged.

While Rhonda dried her face with the stinking sheets, Eddie fumbled onto the bed, positioning himself beside her, and kissed her neck. He caressed her breasts and ran his hand down the length of her leg.

"That was an accident. I swear," he said.

Eddie supposed that Rhonda wanted nothing more than to be as far from him as she could get, but his ministrations slowly turned the tide. Breathless, she eased as Eddie explored her intimate parts. Guiding Rhonda to her hands and knees, Eddie knelt behind her atop the small bed. He struggled to readiness, encouraging himself by hand. As she waited on all fours, Eddie recalled an episode from a long ago trip to Bali. Rhonda appeared as if she might be wondering whether she'd included pot scrubbers in her most recent supplier order.

"Just give me a minute, would you?" Finally, a quiet moan passed from him as he found sufficient rigidity to begin. Rocking gently at first, Eddie entered into a pleasing rhythm.

He thrust away quietly for some time, Rhonda not bothering to feign enthusiasm. As the minutes passed, a lifetime of cigarette smoking constricted his breathing, his attempts at quickening leaving him increasingly gasping for air. Thoughts, fears, and anxiety began to emerge. Would he finish? Would he collapse from exhaustion and the lingering odour of Rhonda's digestive gas? The pursuit became a race against time. Pushing aside the doubts and breathlessness, Eddie persisted with vigour. Thrusting with fury, a sudden shuddering cascaded through him, his body afire. Ecstasy overtook him; oxygen depleted, his muscles spasmed and contracted with his final thrust and ejaculation. Lightning struck. A deep tearing in his left hamstring buckled him forward in searing pain. Throwing himself forward in agony, the full weight of his body crushed Rhonda flat. "Ahhhhh," Eddie screamed in agony and ecstasy, clutching the back of his leg.

"Get the fuck off me!" Rhonda screamed as she heaved to force him off.

Writhing in pain, Eddie did his best to roll away. As he lifted his body ever so slightly, Rhonda's right arm freed up. With a swift elbow, she shoved with all her might as he rolled away. The unexpected shove sent him sprawling to the floor. On the way, his head clipped the edge of the side table, wobbling the nightstand and dislodging the heavy glass ashtray, which struck him squarely on the bridge of his nose and showered him in lipstick-smeared cigarette butts and ashes. Blood gushed from his nostrils as he lay amidst the ashes, clutching his hamstring.

"Oh Jesus!" Rhonda screamed as she struggled to her feet. "Out! Get out!" Rhonda scrambled to gather the pile of Eddie's clothing. Bumping off the bedroom door frame, she carried Eddie's things to the trailer door, dropping a sock along the way. She flung the trailer door open and tossed his clothing down the steps.

Eddie limped along after her. "Rhonda, please. I'm so, so sorry. This is not—"

"Get the fuck out!" Rhonda screamed, stepping aside as the blood from Eddie's broken nose dripped onto her grimy, lime-green shag carpet. "Out!"

Naked Eddie passed naked Rhonda in the doorway, close enough for a large drop of blood to fall from the end of his nose onto her left nipple.

"Jesus fucking Christ, get out!" Rhonda yelled.

Eddie grabbed the rickety metal handrail and hopped down the steps on one foot, as best he could. He gathered his items and struggled to the Rolls, tossing his clothing onto the passenger seat. Wincing from throbbing pain, Eddie lowered his naked body into the driver's seat, thankful that it was his left hamstring and not his right, which surely would have prevented driving. His chest, belly, penis, and thighs now covered in rivulets of blood, Eddie started the engine and placed the Rolls in gear to make his exit.

As the car rolled forward, Rhonda's voice rang out, "Wait! What about Travis?"

CHAPTER 9

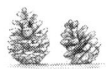

The last of the gaggle of girls said their goodbyes as they wandered off. Melanie loved that they hung around after her lectures. She loved the familiarity of sitting with her students in the front seats of the lecture hall and chatting about the material she'd spoken on. They were fans. She obliged their adoration with bits of wisdom and intrigue about the authors they were reading and the books they wrote. The outtakes of her lectures really.

Melanie gathered up her notes and packed her leather satchel. Plans were in place for a quiet drink with Mo-Chi. She'd lingered too long and needed to be on her way. They met less often now, so it seemed an extra pleasure when they did manage a sit-down. When Melanie first arrived at the college, Mo-Chi Bison had been a much-needed friend. Mo-Chi was now in the waning days of her position as head librarian at the campus library. The two had bonded in the early days of Melanie's return to Casper, which had not been an entirely happy one. There was a gentleness, a comforting energy to Mo-Chi that had allowed Melanie to speak openly and honestly about her ambivalence. Mo-Chi assisted Melanie with locating, retrieving, and ordering books she needed for research. Despite an age gap of more than twenty years, Mo-Chi and Melanie found in one another a kindred spirit.

Their usual table was taken when they arrived at the quiet steak house where they'd shared so many confessional meals. The Roundtable Steak and Potato was a haunt favoured by older professionals looking for an unhurried dinner and drink. The women felt comfortable there. They took seats at a table near the side gallery with floor-to-ceiling windows that captured the majesty of Casper Mountain. It was here that Mo-Chi had shared her struggles about her errant husband, worries about retirement and being overextended with a truck lease, her fears about having to let a junior librarian go. Here, where Melanie had sought comfort after putting Angela into care, where Melanie had told Mo-Chi her life story. Or at least the one she'd come to believe.

A glass of wine and salad suited them. The women got caught up with personal news, talked about the new building going up on campus, and laughed about the trivial politics and tempests among faculty. Melanie laughed and chatted easily with Mo-Chi, but discussion of her father's letters and his invitation were not among the shared items. Melanie knew well enough that Mo-Chi would never countenance the notion of responding to an abandoner. And anyway, Melanie could think of no logical counterargument in support of responding to Eddie. She saw no reason to upset a lovely evening with vexatious banter. In the fifteen or so years she'd known her, Mo-Chi's warmth and nurturing had been a home of sorts for Melanie. Whether passing in the stacks at the library, or over an early morning coffee, with her smile or a quick hug, Mo-Chi had signalled her approval. Now, as the older Mo-Chi braced for retirement and her return to Lame Deer, Montana, Melanie began to consider life without her close at hand.

The women finished their dinner with quick summaries of

the activities of Mo-Chi's daughters, who'd begun busy lives with young children in Butte, Montana; and Eugene, Oregon. Melanie talked about the mud fever Blade was recovering from. Checks were paid and the women said their goodbyes in the parking lot. Melanie drove home in the twilight, hoping there was enough molasses in the barn to assuage Blade's inevitable annoyance. The sound of Melanie's tires on the gravel driveway alerted Blade to her arrival. His loud whinnying conveying irritation. Melanie knew all too well that Blade would make her pay for her inattentiveness. As steady a trail ride as he was, Blade could be petulant. Ambling ever so casually into the barn, Melanie called out in the warmest, most apologetic tone she could muster, "Hi, Blade." Relieved to find a bit of molasses still in the bucket, she approached his stall with the sweet peace offering. After briefly ignoring her, Blade quickly conceded, placing his head into the bucket. She laughed at his quick retreat. Melanie knew his weak spot.

    She led him out of the stall, turned on the paddock light at the door, and let Blade loose. He stretched his legs, cantering round the circular paddock as Melanie watched. She studied his gait and wondered about what ancient lines he'd come from. She saw and felt some earthly tug.

    Melanie quietly groomed Blade in the paddock as a slender crescent moon rose above the Wyoming plain. She loved this time with him in the dark quiet. After she led him in for the night, she hugged his neck, pressing her face to him, deeply breathing his scent. She turned out the lights and walked to her empty house.

    Upstairs in her bedroom, Melanie placed her satchel on the bed and quickly performed her bedtime routine. Finally propped against a pillow in bed, she took her laptop from the satchel and opened it. She sat quietly a moment and clicked on the app she'd signed onto several months earlier.

Melanie's relationships with men had always been the result of chance. It had been an act of curiosity more than anything else to have opened an account on a dating website. The novelty of a marketplace of human flesh wore thin quickly. She'd checked for matches no more than a handful of times in the first several weeks before abandoning the undertaking. It seemed a parade of carnal need, loneliness, and desperation. One she was embarrassed by. Still, she admired the efficiency of it. Melanie listened to the crickets and night sounds as she scrolled through faces. Divorced men, widowed men, lifelong bachelors, none compelling enough to warrant her attention. She swiped away most before closing her laptop.

She sat in quiet reflection, wondering whether this was her fate. To rise in the morning and go to sleep alone for the rest of her days. It was curious, this condition. Certainly, there were yearnings. Needs. Yes, she longed for companionship, support, intimacy. But it came to her that there was something off about her reasons for seeking out dates with men she knew next to nothing about. Other than the fiction of their online bios or the falseness of long-out-of-date pictures, the notion of finding a missing piece this way seemed to Melanie far-fetched at best. She'd known this was the likely outcome before she signed onto the app. Why had she gone looking in this way? And why, when she thought about the whole thing, was she relatively unbothered by the idea of being alone? So little of it made sense to her.

Melanie wondered how Mo-Chi Bison would fare in retirement. What would her day look like? How would she fill her time? She envisioned visiting her in Reserve territory, greeting her at the door of some lovely home Mo-Chi had made. The crickets chirruped outside, and clouds rolled across the night sky as Melanie drifted in these visions. She settled her head on a pillow and thought of the dinners they'd shared, coffees, and the many kindnesses her friend had shown her.

The clouds thickened, and Melanie fell asleep. There, in sleep, the white mare appeared, sparkling under a starlit sky. The mare wandered the western Great Plains. The roan yearling trailed behind. A darkness came. A thick blackness took the sky. The yearling fell further behind, mare receding into fading light on a distancing horizon. The yearling searched, scampering forward, in what direction, she didn't know. Fog rolled across the plain. Mist obscured the stars above, hid the horizon ahead, concealed the path behind. The yearling lay down, astray on the damp earth. The silent darkness prevailed.

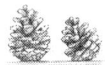

Bits of light broke through tall cedars on the eastern edge of the ranch. Light filtered round the homestead building to the south and west windows of Melanie's bedroom. Her eyes opened slowly. This room she'd known since earliest childhood was alien in her fading dreams. She breathed deeply. Felt the familiar comfort of her bed. Resumed her place among the living. Melanie scrabbled down the bed on her back to stretch her arms out above her. She extended her arms and legs as far as they'd reach. The stretch felt good. Reenergized, she lay in quiet contemplation for a few moments. She needed to pee. Her tummy grumbled with hunger.

Melanie sat up and opened her night table drawer. She retrieved an opened envelope and pulled yellow legal paper from it. She took the second of two letters she'd read more than a dozen times. The words he wrote. Words he wrote to her. His eyes and hand had been on these pages in the way that her eyes and shaking hand were on them now. She was not the seeker, as she'd believed. She was the sought. Melanie scanned for the words, finding them like flickering candles. Words she didn't know she'd longed to see, "you are my daughter, and I am your father."

Chapter 10

The incongruousness of hiking across a muddy forest trail, dressed in a business suit, never occurred to Edward R. Novak. It was just what he did. This day, he wore his least old suit. A suit he could still wear in any downtown law office. With the exception of Eddie's longish grey hair, he might well have passed for any older gentleman. Distinguished older gentleman even.

His hamstring throbbing, nose aching, Eddie limped through the final painful few hundred metres of brush before getting to the drive shed. A few careful steps up the ladder to his cash box and soon enough he was winding his way along the picturesque road through Cailly onward to the big highway. Eddie took with him a thick stack of fifty- and hundred-dollar-bills. He'd arrange his winter stay in Huntsville and stock up on items for his final weeks at the cabin—the duration of his autumn tenure there being measured by his tolerance for a cold lake bath. Eddie was an outdoorsman but not willing to risk hypothermia by placing himself in the lake in November. Moreover, a single night too long at the cabin could prove disastrous. An unexpected snowfall could strand him indefinitely.

The rest of today's events were all meticulously choreographed.

Everything. His arrival at the courthouse, his cover story, the delicate points of entry into the conversation about Travis's case, the carefully constructed artifice of his desire to be of some simple assistance. All of it, a complete fabrication. Of course, there was the possibility of unplanned circumstances and interlopers with agendas of their own that needed to be worked around. This was territory Edward R. Novak had navigated for half a century. There were few if any situations that Eddie hadn't ad libbed his way around or out of. But before all that, he had business of his own to attend to.

The parking lot of the Blu-Jay Motel looked as forlorn as ever. Tucked away on the edge of Huntsville beneath creaky old pines, with its weeds and scrub grass well on their way to reclaiming the parking area, the two-storey white clapboard affair was the most unremarkable building in town. The Blu-Jay's only saving grace might have been its quiet location and sleep-inducing signage. Eddie pulled the Rolls right to the door of the management office. This would be his third overwintering here since his humiliating exit from the big city. He'd come to know the proprietors well enough to consider them friends of a sort. Though several years Eddie's junior, Gus and Helen Papadopoulos seemed unusually elderly to him. Running a motel for forty-five years had been more prematurely aging than he might have imagined. Regardless, Eddie appreciated their keen willingness to deal in cash.

Something was amiss. A fresh-faced young girl looked up from behind the front desk as Eddie made his entry through the door. The young woman was a far cry from haggard Gus or his exhausted wife, Helen.

"Good morning," said Eddie. Whatever surprise Eddie might have been experiencing was equally matched by the girl's alarm.

An old man in a business suit with a broken nose, two black eyes, and stringy grey hair was more than a little out of her ordinary day.

"Morning. So, like, do you want something?" the young woman replied, looking up from her phone.

"Edward Novak, pleased to meet you."

"I'm Taylor. Do you, like, want a room?"

"Lovely meeting you, Taylor," said Eddie. "Yes, something like that. I'm a bit of a long-term resident here. I don't remember seeing you before."

"No. I'm new. I've only been here since, like, July."

"I see. Well, I usually make arrangements with Gus, Mr. Papadopoulos, for my winter accommodations. Is he or Helen on-site today?"

"Um . . . Mrs. Papadopoulos only comes in on, like, Mondays and Thursdays now. And uh-um . . ." Taylor stammered a moment.

"Yes?" Eddie intervened.

"Mr. Papadopoulos passed away," Taylor announced.

"Oh my goodness. That's . . . That's very sad and unfortunate."

"Oh yeah, Mrs. P. has been, like, struggling. She's like, mega-sad all the time now. Mr. P. was, like, a big part of the community."

"Well, I'll have to speak with her when I see her next. For the time being, I wondered if you could book me in from the last week of October through the first week of April."

"Um. I've never, like, booked anyone for that long before. So . . . I dunno. Does Mrs. P., like, give you a special rate or something?"

"Yes, something like that."

"The computer doesn't let me book more than two weeks at a time. I guess I could, like, reregister you after the two weeks. Maybe I should talk to Mrs. P."

"What I'm going to do is give you some money now, and you can do what you need to do with Helen, Mrs. Papadopoulos. If you just tell her Eddie's coming for the winter, she'll know what to do. Okay?"

"Oh, okay, Mr. Novak. I'll, like, do that then."

Eddie produced a folded wad of bills from his suit jacket pocket. "Do you know the combination to the safe?"

"Oh yeah, I do."

"Okay, very good, so I'm going to give you some money now, and what I'd like you to do is put it into the safe straight away, all right?"

"Okay. I guess."

"But before we do that," Eddie said, "I'm going to count this money out, and you can print me a receipt for it."

"But don't I have to, like, book the room first to print out a receipt?"

"No, that's not necessary. Helen, Mrs. Papadopoulos, will take care of those arrangements. For now, just write a receipt by hand that you received this money, all right?"

"I'm not sure. I don't know if I'm supposed to do this."

"Do what, dear?"

"Like . . . um, take money."

"Taylor, this motel is still an operating business, right?"

"*Operating* like a hospital operation?"

Gathering himself for a moment as the blood rushed to his head, Eddie reconsidered his approach while calming himself.

"No, no, that's not what I mean. I'm asking if the motel is still functioning. As in, does the motel still take guests?"

"Duh, yeah," mystified Taylor retorted.

"All right then. Good. And now, Taylor, you understand that a business, just like this one, takes money from paying customers, right?"

"Well, yeah."

"And you know that these bills are money, right?"

"Um, yeah . . . like, I guess."

"You guess? Okay, anyway, look, I'm just going to count out this money. You're going to put it in the safe behind you, but first, write 'received' on a piece of paper with '$6000.00' and your initials. Okay?"

"Whatever." Taylor sighed. After initialling and handing over the receipt, Taylor placed the money into the safe.

"Thank you, Taylor. It was very special, like, meeting you," said Eddie.

"Uh huh," Taylor responded as she resumed her phone scrolling.

Eddie returned to the safety of the Rolls-Royce Corniche. He sat for a moment and wondered how he would survive Taylor. October to April was a long stretch. Though he'd tried very hard in his life never to underestimate the inadvertent genius of truly stupid people, Eddie found his encounter with Taylor a deeply discouraging indicator of the human condition. Eddie started the Rolls, cruised across the secondary arteries, and glided down the main drag into town. He needed to pop into the health food store to pick up his supplements before hustling over to the grocery store.

The parking gods favoured him this day. An open space on Main Street hadn't been a sure thing in Huntsville for years. Finding an open parking spot directly in front of the door brought a wide smile to Eddie's face. Though no lover of jazz, Eddie didn't find the overhead bebop in the health food emporium offensive in any way. It recollected for him the old music business adage about pop musicians playing three chords to 10,000 people, and jazz musicians playing 10,000 chords to three people. In some strange way, in this most unlikely of locations, Eddie's predisposition toward the melancholia of minor chords seemed in retreat ever so briefly.

It wasn't like Eddie to groove to anything upbeat, and yet, he found himself tapping a toe in the checkout line with his beetroot and ginseng. Eddie couldn't account for the unexpected cheerful impulse. He finished paying and got on his way down the road to the grocery store.

Eddie recoiled momentarily from the artificial glare of the white-hot lighting. It was arresting but effective in its purpose. The produce seemed alive; packaged goods seemed to gleam; floors, fixtures, and shelves appeared clean and sparkling. A far cry from Rhonda's grubby and dim Mercantile. Eddie scanned the rows and rows of items. He scoffed to himself. Crap. All of it, complete and total crap. Empty calories, sugar, and chemicals of every known sort. Eddie headed for the edges as he always did in these places. Meat and vegetables. Beyond that, he had little interest. Eddie's subtle moral superiority about his diet existed in blithe opposition to his problematic drinking and lifelong smoking habit.

Eddie made quick work of picking up a steak, sausages, red and yellow peppers, two potatoes, sour cream, some expensive coffee, butter, and eggs. The freshness was a pleasant change from Rhonda's dreary goods. He contemplated the size of his fridge and the number of items he was purchasing. He'd need as many items as his fridge space would allow. It was immediately apparent to Eddie before he'd reached the end of Rhonda's driveway, he would not be a welcome sight at the Mercantile for quite some time.

The efficiency, eye contact, and pleasant greeting from the concerned-looking cashier thrilled Eddie. The notion of a sentient adult checking his items and taking his money seemed a novel encounter. He loaded his grocery items into the back seat and checked his pocket watch for the time. He admired its gold casing and the engraved back: "Congratulations on Your Retirement, Jerome." Eddie was reasonably sure Jerome and his surviving children would have wanted him to have this watch. Regardless, it was Eddie's now.

Eddie knew well enough that a 1:30 conference time would be the first docket item after the lunch break. The presiding judge would return between 1:10 and 1:15. Ms. Mulgrave would be on-site no later than 1:20. The exquisite timepiece said it was 12:45. More than enough time to make it over to Chaffey Street.

Eddie drove slowly through town to the courthouse, circled the tree-lined block once, and parked on a street beside the building. He positioned the Rolls beneath a mid-sized maple tree such that he could see the staff entrance and small parking areas to the front and side of the courthouse. Here he lay in wait. Reclining his seat slightly, checking his timepiece—1:03, perfect—Eddie made himself comfortable. Sitting in repose and admiring a cluster of dusty rose sedum plants on the front garden of the tiny home across the street, Eddie hummed the opening sweep of Barber's Adagio for Strings.

As the minutes passed, Eddie drifted in visions of Melanie at play. Despite his occasional searches, Eddie had never found her likeness online. Was she disfigured in some way? Was it just by chance that her photo had never been posted anywhere? Had she been diligent in avoiding dissemination of photos of herself? Was it her own father from whom she'd wanted to shelter her appearance? It was a recurring frustration that he couldn't conjure her visage any other way than the twenty-two-month-old child she'd been. These well-travelled thoughts occupied him.

As he fixed his gaze ahead, a car approached from behind. Catching the corner of his eye as it passed, the late model grey sedan slowed to turn into the side parking lot. An upscale ride without flash. The driver pulled into the reserved spot by the side door. Confirmation of his carefully considered expectation. His quarry was in sight. He moved without hesitation, opening his door and hobbling with as much purpose as he could, up and over the lawn embankment into the lot. He watched as the driver's door opened. A tall, elegantly dressed man appeared, by this point no more than a handful of metres from Eddie.

The elusive thrill of merciless killing rose up in Edward R. Novak. His prey was known. Coincidence had smiled on Eddie. Immediately calculating the necessary nonchalance, Eddie baited his old ally into the moment of discovery by awaiting a predictable greeting.

"Eddie?" the gentleman asked with great surprise.

"John?!" Eddie called with convincing delight. Eddie took Judge John D. Hathaway's extended hand and gripped it firmly.

"Nice to see you, Eddie. It's been years. What brings you all the way up here?" Judge Hathaway asked.

"Oh hell, John. You know I've been coming up here since the dawn of time," said Eddie.

"Jesus, Eddie," said Judge Hathaway, "what in the world has happened to your face? Look at you."

"Oh, for the love of God, John. The enormity of my embarrassment. Please don't make me explain." Eddie produced a mischievous grin.

"Hahaha, I can only imagine," said Judge Hathaway.

"I see from the parking spot, you're still on the bench," said Eddie.

"Still at it. I really need to pack it in. I just can't seem to let it go. Jesus, what'll become of me if I do?"

"What becomes of any of us, I guess," Eddie commiserated.

"I did pull the plug four years ago, but they're so short on benchers, they asked me to come back and do circuit stuff in these far-out places. I was done for about six months and bored out of my mind, so I thought, what the hell, I'll do it. Last week I was in Atikokan. Next week, I'm in Sharbot Lake. Silly really, at my age."

"How are Jeannie and the boys?" Eddie asked.

"Oh shit, Jeannie's furious with me. As usual. No news there. She's fine. She's got Michael's kids three days a week. They can't get decent daycare where they are. She's filling in. Michael's good. Working his tail off, wholesaling tools to the big box stores. Danny bounces around from thing to thing. Last week I counted, he's had four jobs in the last seven years. The thing is, he keeps making better dough, so maybe I should keep my mouth shut about that," said John.

"I ran into Rob Miller several months ago, and he said something similar about his daughter having a resume like a bloody Tolstoy novel," Eddie said.

"Hey, listen, I've got a conference in twenty minutes. If you've got time, pop into chambers with me for a quick catch-up. What are you in town for?"

There it was. An invitation to dance. And Edward R. Novak would oblige. Of course, he would. John Hathaway was an old friend. Eddie had been assigned as John's articling principal more than forty years ago. In those days, Eddie was a rigorous practitioner with a healthy appreciation for the traditions of the legal trade and had a firm grasp of the practical aspects of law. In fact, Edward R. Novak was a sought-after mentor for any candidate to the bar. Whatever rough edges he might have had, he remained an excellent instructor.

As was the case in Eddie's life, good things didn't last. Within weeks of the assignment, the pair had forged a kind of unholy bond. An occasional drink after work quickly became a regular feature of their week. The two had found in one another a mutual fondness for alcohol, illicit substances, and women. What was in its origins a reasonable, albeit informal, style of providing guidance ultimately became something other than instructional. Or at least not instructional where the practice of law was concerned. Late-night merrymaking, carousing, and simultaneous intimacy with shared partners was not precisely within the firm's expectations when the articling assignment was made.

"I do have some appointments I must get to, but sure, let's," said Eddie.

"Great. Come on in. I won't keep you," said John as the pair turned for the staff entrance. With its terrazzo floor, walls in safe colours, and functional handrail up well-worn stairs, the courthouse smelled of bureaucracy and administrivia. The pair made their way up the stairs to chambers, and then Judge Hathaway led Eddie down the second-storey hall to a broad oak door. Eddie dispensed with any survey of the room. Chambers here were not unlike chambers anywhere. Wood-panelled walls, mahogany desk, shelves of law books, padded leather chairs. Eddie took one of two seats in front of the desk as John placed himself behind it.

"Are you before the court today?" Judge Hathaway asked.

"Goodness no, John. I haven't practised in a couple of years." It appeared Judge Hathaway had not heard of Eddie's recent suspension and final disqualification. Or if he had, he was being polite.

"What brings you in?" asked John.

"Minor property matter. Nothing earth-shaking." Eddie shrugged. "And what about you? What's on the docket?"

"God have mercy, Eddie. Some piece of shit blew his shed up or something out in the middle of nowhere. I don't know," said John. "You mentioned running into Rob Miller. I haven't talked to him in . . . gotta be four or five years. How's he keeping? Still with those other clowns?" asked John.

"Oh, Johnny, I try not to ask too many questions with him. I'd heard it around that he was fighting with one of the other partners. Something about money and not making his billings. As far as I know, he's still with the other guys. I don't know though."

The two happily gossiped about old work colleagues and former clients for several minutes. Eddie discreetly checked the time before launching into memories of their personal history. Miss Mulgrave was past her expected arrival, and he needed to quickly but naturally establish a more intimate tone with John.

". . . well let's be honest, Hathaway, I don't think either of us were the same after Cabo San Lucas," Eddie suggested with a conspiratorial smile.

"Jesus, that was awful. Really, really awful."

"Oh, nonsense. You loved it. You bloody well started the whole thing," Eddie laughed.

"I think you're right. The tequila. Shit. That was way off the rails," said John.

"I'm telling you, that guy on the beach you got the stuff from . . . I don't know what it was," said Eddie, shaking his head, "but it wasn't what he said it was."

"What were we thinking?" John shook his head.

"I never told you, Judith threatened to bring all of that up in our divorce," said Eddie.

"Can you blame her? Jeannie said Judith never shut up about it on the plane ride home. I don't even want to tell you what Jeannie said she'd do if I ever pulled a stunt like that again. But

I mean, seriously, Eddie. Those Mexican ladies. Disaster," said John.

The trip down memory lane came to an abrupt end with a crisp knock on the door. "Shit, that's my pre-trial. Sorry, Eddie, I gotta wrap this up." John tipped his chair upright and gathered some folders.

"Okay, old friend, let me get out of your hair. We'll catch up further another time," Eddie said, rising to leave.

"We'll do that," said John as he rounded the desk to escort Eddie to the door. The men quietly shook hands and said their goodbyes at the door before Judge Hathaway opened it to let Eddie out. There on the other side of the doorway, a respectful distance back, stood victim number two.

Karen Mulgrave smiled and nodded to the men. As Eddie stepped out into the hallway, Judge Hathaway invited Miss Mulgrave in. "Miss Mulgrave, welcome. Do come in." As she stepped around him, Eddie gave only the subtlest glance before addressing her.

"Miss Mulgrave? Karen Mulgrave?" he asked.

"Yes. That's right. I'm sorry, have we met?"

"Oh my goodness! Your Honour, I can't tell you the deep debt of gratitude I owe this extraordinary young woman," said Eddie, looking to John.

"Thank you. I'm sorry. I'm . . . I'm just having trouble placing . . ." Karen Mulgrave stammered.

"Your Honour, if you'll allow it, and I certainly don't want to take up more of your time, but if I could just tell you very briefly about Miss Mulgrave's kindness."

"Please do," said John, curiously.

"This is going back several years. I'd had an unfortunate episode with a critically ill family member. The minutes were evaporating as he lay dying. In a harried attempt to get to the hospital to see him through his final minutes, I drove in a manner not befitting an officer of the court. Hearing my story, Miss Mulgrave was incredibly gracious in withdrawing the charges. I really cannot thank you enough, Miss Mulgrave, and I assure you, your generosity has not been forgotten," said Eddie.

"That's wonderful. Miss Mulgrave, I think you've made a life-long friend in Mr. Novak," said John.

"Yes. Yes, of course. I'm sorry, Mr. Novak. Of course. I remember you now. I was just having a moment there. I didn't recognize you. It seems you've had a spot of trouble," said Karen, with a nod to his injured face.

"Yes, Miss Mulgrave, aging is not for the faint of heart, I promise you that. We're all a little unsteady on our feet. Well, what a pleasure to see you again," said Eddie.

"And you as well, Mr. Novak," said Karen.

"Please. Call me Eddie. Everyone does. 'Mr. Novak' makes me sound ancient."

"You are ancient, and I've heard you called any number of other things, none of them 'Eddie,'" said John to the amusement of his audience.

The trio stood laughing in the pleasing glow of bonhomie. The moment had arrived. He had his quarry squarely in sight. Shared memories, confessional trust, conviviality, ingratiating flattery all perfectly in place. Edward R. Novak would cast his line and see what he might land.

"Look, friends, I've taken up enough of your time. I should run," said Eddie.

"No rush. Unfortunately, I was only coming to notify His Honour that our defendant hasn't appeared as yet," said Karen.

"Did he notify your office or the court clerk?" asked Judge Hathaway.

"Not that I'm aware," said Karen.

"All right, we'll give him a few more minutes," said Judge Hathaway.

"And so, Mr.—Eddie, are you before the court today?" asked Karen.

"No. No. Nothing like that. I'm just here on a property matter. Nothing dramatic by any means," said Eddie.

"Are you up here full-time now, Eddie?" asked John.

"I am actually. I have a place in a little hamlet no one's ever heard of just north of here," said Eddie.

"Where's that?" asked Karen.

"Cailly. It's just outside the western edge of the park, up Highway 11."

"Oh, that's where our defendant is from," said Karen. Eddie's bait had been taken precisely as planned.

"Is that right?" asked Eddie.

"I thought the police report indicated Perry Township," said John.

"Yes, that would fit. Cailly is in Perry Township," said Eddie.

"Anyway, I suspect this one's going to be a no-show, so if you gentleman would like to carry on your meeting, I won't interrupt further," said Karen.

"A no-show?" Eddie prodded.

"Sadly, I don't think he'll be appearing today," said Karen.

"Wouldn't be the first one," finished Judge Hathaway

"Look, ah . . . without wanting to intrude in any way, could I gently inquire, is this related to an explosion of a trailer several weeks back?" asked Eddie.

"It is, yes," Karen confirmed.

"Probably big news in the township, I'd guess," said John.

"Again, certainly no intention to intrude here, but I do have some information that may assist the court in this matter. Well, perhaps *assist* is an overstatement, but I can tell you with a degree of confidence, your defendant will not be appearing today," Eddie informed them.

"I think it might be best if we took this into chambers," said Judge Hathaway in a hushed tone. The three retreated into chambers and took seats.

"All right, Eddie, Mr. Novak, if you'd like to share information that you feel is pertinent, I'm certainly happy to listen, pending the Crown's agreement," said Judge Hathaway seated at his desk and folding his hands together before him.

"I have no objection, presuming the information is not prejudicial to the Crown's case," said Karen. If Karen Mulgrave had any inkling as to Eddie's disbarment, it wasn't immediately apparent. After recollecting his name and her experience with him, she certainly would have connected recent newspaper reports or tittle-tattle of his disbarment. Odds on, she likely had. But if she had, why did she ask if he was before the court today? Was she mocking him by suggesting he might be before the court as a defendant? Wouldn't she advance objections to these sorts of conversations on the basis of his disgrace? Eddie noted and silently admired her impressive inscrutability.

"Let me just make clear, I don't see myself in any formal role of *amicus curiae* here," said Eddie, leaning back in the chair he'd taken. "I don't think it rises to that level. The information I have bears no grand significance. I offer it just in hope of saving both of you some time."

"I have no objection in that case," said Karen.

"All right then, out with it, Mr. Novak," instructed Judge Hathaway.

"As I said, no grand significance, but I can tell you, the individual I believe you're waiting for is currently in Guelph, Ontario, with no definite return date," advised Eddie.

"Guelph?" asked Judge Hathaway.

"Yes, more than that I can't say," said Eddie. This was Edward R. Novak taking flight. From the moment Rhonda told him where Travis was, Eddie knew full well how he'd use that information to his advantage. He had good reason to anticipate what inferences the Crown and a judge would draw if the information was presented in a certain way, in a certain context.

Guelph was home to an excellent and renowned addiction treatment facility. Certainly, some people in legal circles might easily intuit, or even conclude, that a defendant visiting Guelph would be seeking treatment for drug or alcohol addiction. And yes, such people might infer from Eddie's reluctance to discuss Travis's visit to Guelph that Eddie may have been concerned for personal health confidentiality. It didn't matter that Travis Smith was likely in a rat-infested back alley, smoking methamphetamine. So long as Eddie didn't say that Travis was in Guelph receiving addiction treatment, he hadn't technically lied.

"Does he have family or associates in Guelph that we could contact?" asked Karen.

"No, I don't believe so. My understanding is that he's there for personal reasons," said Eddie.

"I see. All right, I think we can gather from that what might be underway. Thank you, Eddie . . . Mr. Novak," said Judge Hathaway.

"As far as I know, the young man has led an enormously difficult life. I'm sure you can imagine," said Eddie, invitingly.

"Difficult or not, running a meth lab is a choice," said Karen, fluttering with moral certitude.

"Allegedly running a meth lab," said Judge Hathaway.

"His failure to appear isn't alleged," said Karen.

"For the moment anyway," cautioned Judge Hathaway.

"Your Honour, these are dual procedure charges . . ." began Karen.

"I'm aware of how the charges are brought, but it seems unreasonable to forthwith go down the rabbit hole of arguments about failure to appear, unnecessary delay, et cetera, given what we know about the defendant," countered Judge Hathaway, presumptively.

"Miss Mulgrave, it seems to me, you may be diminishing your own case by pushing on the defendant's absence today," the judge advised.

"Your Honour, the defendant has taken up the court's time by his inability or unwillingness to appoint counsel, and by failing to notify our office or the court clerk that he would not be present here today," pleaded Karen, straightening the collar of her skirt suit.

"Look, dear friends, I think this may be my cue to exit. It was not my intention to set the cat amongst the pigeons, so to speak, and you obviously have a serious matter before you, so I'm happy to leave you to sort this out," said Eddie, making no effort to remove himself.

"Your Honour, if Mr. Novak has information that may be helpful to us in contacting the defendant, or at least confirming his availability, the Crown would be grateful for his assistance," said Karen, smiling in hopeful anticipation.

"Miss Mulgrave, I'm here on an unrelated matter. It was strictly by chance that I've run into my old colleague, Judge Hathaway," said Eddie noncommittally.

"Is the defendant known to you, Mr. Novak?" Judge Hathaway asked.

"Yes, he certainly is. However, as I said, the information I've provided is offered solely to assist procedurally," Eddie suggested.

"Your Honour, the defendant has been incommunicado since the inception of this matter, and I've had no end of difficulty reaching him or any appointed counsel." Karen let her gesticulating hand drop to her lap in frustration.

"Look, Eddie, if you can help us move the ball down the field, or at least point us in the right direction here, I can't speak for Miss Mulgrave, but I know I'd certainly appreciate it," Judge Hathaway said.

"Well, I sense the urgency and insistence, so I'm happy to provide you what I know," said Eddie with a grave nod.

"If you could just give us some background, the court would be grateful," said Judge Hathaway.

A Crown prosecutor and a judge practically begging for his participation in a legal proceeding after he'd been disbarred. Eddie contained his impulse to smile. Whether Eddie's old friend or the Crown were aware of his recent disbarment remained unclear. It was possible that both of their inquiries about him being before the court were simply sly entry points for Eddie to bring the topic up himself. If that had been the case, he hadn't taken the bait. Regardless, he'd been invited into the conversation, and that was all that mattered. The execution of his endgame was at hand.

"I'm not aware of what specific charges have been brought, but I'm sure you can imagine the defendant is more to be pitied than vilified. It's my understanding that he has struggled with the same affliction that so many of our young people have. Young Travis has repeatedly appeared in town in a state of deep distress and is the object of scorn and ridicule among locals," said Eddie. "I'm told his people are originally from North Bay, but he and his mother spent more than a decade in the city of Hamilton," Eddie continued.

"Be that as it may, Mr. Smith is facing very serious charges. Production of a Controlled Substance, Mischief Endangering Life, Arson by Negligence, Criminal Negligence, and Possession for the Purpose of Trafficking," said Karen, leaning in toward the judge's desk.

"Good heavens! Yes, serious indeed. Well, I suppose I shouldn't be surprised by all of it. Young Travis never really had a father, and as far as I know, he's been quite unfortunate in his search for positive role models. According to many, he's been the victim of more than one unsavoury influence. It's all so sad, not just for the community at large but also for his dear mother. As I understand it, Mr. Smith resides on property owned by his mother, who I can tell you is a very upstanding, and dare I say it, outstanding member of what is a tight little community. It pains me to think she may be affected by all of this. My heart goes out to the poor woman," said Eddie, shaking his head gravely.

"The kid sounds like a bloody menace," said John.

"Your Honour, from what I understand, the defendant is a twenty-eight-year-old man," countered Karen.

"Was it his mother's place he blew up?" asked Judge Hathaway.

"No, Your Honour, the police report indicates that she was in separate living quarters but that there was considerable smoke damage to her mobile home, or trailer, I'm not sure which," said Karen.

Folding his arms across his chest, Judge Hathaway looked to the ceiling and sat in quiet contemplation before inquiring. "Other than the mother's place, were there any neighbouring structures damaged?" continued Judge Hathaway.

"Not to my knowledge, Your Honour," Karen noted.

"Being familiar with the area, I can tell you the two live in what can only be described as rather lonesome isolation. There isn't another building for several kilometres. Sadly, the mother's valiant attempts to get her son help have been limited by their isolation and meagre circumstances," said Eddie.

"Meagre or not, meth labs are a major challenge for local authorities, Your Honour," said Karen.

"I'm aware of the challenges. Look, Miss Mulgrave, is there no way you could get in touch with the defendant's mother or some responsible representative and come to some understanding about the serious nature of what he's alleged to have been involved in?" asked Judge Hathaway.

"Your Honour, I have tried repeatedly to reach the defendant. I was hoping that perhaps through Mr. Novak we'd be able to connect with Mr. Smith without having to go through formal failure to appear steps that would only complicate the matter," said Karen.

"Thank you, Miss Mulgrave. I think that's both prudent and considerate of the court's time. But of course, that places the court at the willingness of an uninvolved third party to act in the public interest. Mr. Novak is under absolutely no obligation to assist here," said Judge Hathaway.

"John, please, we've been friends for forty years. Of course, I'll assist. It's no trouble at all for me to attend his mother's location and encourage her to understand the seriousness of all of this. And certainly, encourage her to communicate to her son that the court is not his enemy, and that whatever shame he's inevitably feeling would be mitigated by standing before the court and accepting responsibility for whatever youthful indiscretions he may be responsible for," said Eddie.

The trivialization of charges being just another in Edward R. Novak's bag of tricks, Eddie knew full well what reaction he'd be provoking, and equally well, how effective such provocation would be in opening the door to a de facto defence of Mr. Travis Smith.

"With all due respect, Mr. Novak, I don't know that I'd characterize these charges as 'youthful indiscretions,'" countered Karen, turning to face him directly.

"I think that's fair. Though having knowledge of the defendant, I'd be hard pressed to believe he had either the knowledge or organizational skills to commit the offences he's accused of. Whatever he might have been involved in, I suspect it may have been a rather pathetic attempt to serve some need or craving of his own," said Eddie.

"Karen, for the love of God, the kid's a half track, living in the woods. No one was hurt. They live in trailers. He's in Guelph cleaning up. I'm just telling you, if Judge Moser catches this case and has to sit through a three-week trial, she will not look kindly on that kind of inflexibility," cautioned Judge Hathaway.

"Your Honour, the police report clearly indicates that there were chemical compounds, residue, production, and packaging materials on-site. The same fact pattern has been present in many convictions of similar circumstance," insisted Karen.

"I've read the report," sighed Judge Hathaway.

"If I may comment, Your Honour?" Eddie broached.

"Yes, Mr. Novak," a wearied Judge Hathaway agreed.

"It's gone around the community that the police were not in attendance at the scene until three hours after the event."

"Your Honour, I'm uncomfortable pursuing this further. The defendant is absent and unrepresented," Karen intoned.

"Your concerns are heard, Miss Mulgrave. Is this in fact the case? I'd have to check the report on that. And was there some specific reason for bringing this to the court's attention, Mr. Novak?" Judge Hathaway proceeded.

"Yes, Your Honour. As yourself and the Crown are no doubt very aware, a benign fire ensued after a small ignition within a private residence. It's my understanding that several of the local volunteer firefighters, who easily quelled the flames that day, are not trained for this type of alleged event," Eddie pointed out.

"I'm sorry, the relevance of this is what?" asked Crown Prosecutor Mulgrave.

"Look, Miss Mulgrave, far be it from me to weigh in on this, but just having some knowledge of the defendant, the area he lives in, and the community dynamic, I think it may be of some use to the course of justice to understand the obstacles here," said Eddie.

"Eddie, I think you may be straying into territory that's better left to Mr. Smith's legal counsel. If he ever manages to retain one," said an exasperated Judge Hathaway.

"I'm not sure what obstacles you're referring to, Mr. Novak," said Karen.

"As I said, it's clearly not my place to insert myself here, however, in the interest of the court's time, I think it's my responsibility as a concerned citizen to point out certain things," Eddie coaxed.

"Certain things?" asked Karen.

"Well, sure. Look, I suppose if I were a prosecutor, given the police services' failure to respond in a timely way, I'd wonder about little things, like contamination of a crime scene."

"Are you personally aware of any inference of contamination?" Karen inquired.

"Oh, I wouldn't say that, but I mean, you've got a bunch of

local volunteer firefighters with no experience and unknown histories marching around what might be a crime scene and not a police officer anywhere near the place for several hours." Eddie shrugged, suggesting the problem was obvious.

"Unless there's some representation that crime scene contamination occurred, I'm not sure that's relevant," contested an affronted Karen Mulgrave.

"Of course, yes. And please know, my commentary is not by any means representation as the court knows it. Really my only concern here would be that the Crown might present the court with easily defeated positions," suggested Eddie.

"Mr. Novak, the Crown's position is strong. I have no concerns in that regard," Karen said, her lips forming a thin line.

"Sure. And I'm certainly not suggesting anything other than that. I just think in the interest of the court's time, well, I'm reminded of *Boucher*. It's only the Crown's purview to press evidence to its greatest strength, rather than seeking conviction. In this case against an individual, who as I say, is more appropriately pitied than vilified," said Eddie.

"Okay, look, in your estimation, Ed, what do you see as obstacles to the Crown's position?" asked Judge Hathaway. "It seems to me, they've got strong if not very strong evidence on their side."

"Excuse me, Your Honour, I'm not convinced that it's my place to weigh in here. But if you're asking, and the Crown is amenable to an unsolicited point of view, I'd be flattered to provide whatever my opinion's worth."

"With great respect for your esteemed colleague, I don't see the value here, Your Honour," Karen Mulgrave gently protested.

"Karen, it's an informal, off-the-record chat. No one's holding anyone to anything," Judge Hathaway advised.

Raising her hands in exasperation, Karen conceded, "All right, I'm happy to listen."

"Again, no intention toward an unreasonable or unwelcome insertion of myself here. I just feel that the Crown may want to concern itself with all of those trivial little bits of business that sometimes collectively add up to the establishment of reasonable doubt," cautioned Eddie.

"For instance?" asked Judge Hathaway.

"Well, I'm certainly no chemist . . ." With that, Judge John Hathaway smirked and only half succeeded in concealing outward laughter as Eddie continued, "but I would be hesitant in this day and age to be introducing evidence concerning chemical compounds, residues, and so forth."

"Why so?" Karen inquired.

"In my experience, they're cumbersome bits of evidence. And of course, you'd be relying on experts that don't always speak in language that judges and juries understand. You know, all of the ordinary concerns any prosecutor would have. Cross-contamination, false positives, questionable science, incomplete tests, random statistical error, continuity of evidence. Is the Crown aware of how the evidence was collected and transported? Were the personnel conducting collection, transport, and testing qualified? Would any of them withstand defence cross-examination? Anyway, I'm sure you've been through these issues and are standing firm. I admire your resolve."

"Resolve?" asked Karen.

"Yes, *resolve*. I think any competent defence counsel would bring all of this to the fore. And I'm sure a dozen other nettlesome aspects, that as mentioned sometimes have a way of adding up to reasonable doubt," Eddie warned.

"Nettlesome aspects?" Judge Hathaway nudged.

"Sure. Yes. Nettlesome in as much as the only alleged victim in all of it seems to be a damaged old trailer in the middle of the bush. As I understand it, the defendant was not present at the time of the disruption and was nowhere near the scene. That could of course prove difficult in terms of the specific charges regarding negligence of any sort. I just mean to say, there's no way of determining what state the place was in when he left the trailer, and no way of knowing whether the premises were accessed by anyone else in his absence. I mean, if there were volatile compounds present, and I don't know that there were, a mischievous person, or even squirrel or chipmunk or other little woodland creature may have entered and wreaked all manner of havoc, knocking things about and so forth."

"Woodland creatures?" Karen asked, incredulous.

"Sure. But look, that's the least of my thoughts. I mean, if it were me prosecuting, I think the first thing I'd be looking for would be evidence on the defendant, or more precisely, in the defendant. Unless I'm hopelessly ill-informed, community gossip being what it is, my understanding is that the defendant wasn't apprehended and charged for several weeks after the alleged offence. If in fact that is the case, and I'm not asking the Crown to disclose evidence, I just wonder how the Crown might have blood sample or surface evidence of any of the chemical compounds that surely would have been in or on his person the day of the alleged offence."

"Eddie, the trailer didn't blow itself up," Judge Hathaway admonished.

"Unless you've got eyewitness accounts of the defendant at the scene, and physical evidence of his presence at the scene, apparently it did. Now, does that mean there wasn't carelessness involved? Of course not. Clearly, there was some careless storage of something or other, but I think we can all agree that hardly amounts to arson of any sort or the kind of reckless negligence that's being alleged here. Ordinary mischief certainly, but I think what he's been charged with might be a high hill to climb, or maybe a hill that's not entirely worth climbing in view of the young fellow as a sympathetic person and the relatively minor consequences to property. Shabby property, I might add."

"And the possession? How exactly is that explained away?" Miss Mulgrave wondered, positioning her index finger against her right cheek.

"Possession of what specifically? I assume you've got evidence of actual prepared contraband, rather than an ordinary assortment of commonly used household items," Eddie rebutted.

"Was there crack or meth or whatever it was on scene? Can someone remind me?" Judge Hathaway said, flipping pages of his briefing notes.

"Well, not exactly finished, but the components for meth anyway," said Karen.

"Nasal decongestant? Drain cleaner? Nail polish remover? Batteries? This is what you're pressing as best evidence with these charges? I've probably got two or three of those items in my car. These are indictable offences? Well, I wish you the best," said Eddie, shaking his head.

"Your Honour, with the greatest respect for Mr. Novak and his opinions, the Crown will be proceeding with all charges," Crown Prosecutor Mulgrave stated.

"I see. Well, I don't blame you, Miss Mulgrave. The police and your office work very diligently and carefully before bringing charges. Though I wouldn't entirely discount Mr. Novak's concerns," said Judge Hathaway.

Not content with the degree of equivocation from his old

comrade, Eddie quickly calculated another approach. Neither Karen Mulgrave nor John Hathaway had any stake in the final outcome for Travis Smith. It made no difference to either of them what became of him. What was required was for the stakes, the heat, to be elevated, if not for both, then at least the one who would influence the other.

"I think that's a wise position, Your Honour. I agree. The police and Crown are very assiduous in their work. Miss Mulgrave, sometime I must share with you the early wisdom Judge Hathaway showed when the two of us were young men in a variety of different circumstances and locations. As long as I've known him, he's had an amazing knack for knowing just the right position to take," said Eddie with the sincerest smile.

"Look at the time. My goodness. Ed, you mentioned you've got appointments. We have no desire to keep you from them. So, I think we've established some background. Helpful background, thank you, Mr. Novak. And uh . . . so that should wrap it up," Judge Hathaway concluded. Eddie had made clear his interest in the matter. He'd known John long enough to know that further insinuation about their mutual past was not necessary. Judge Hathaway would act accordingly.

"Agreed. And let me just thank you again, Miss Mulgrave, for your kindness those many months ago. I wish you the very best with Mr. Smith's case. I know better than anyone how satisfying a court victory can be. I'll do what I can to have Mr. Smith or competent representation contact you," said Eddie, rising to leave.

"Thank you, and it was a pleasure meeting you again, Mr. Novak. Eddie," said Karen, clearly eager to see his exit.

"You know, Miss Mulgrave, in my many decades before the court, the thing I came to discover is that nothing is guaranteed. It's poker, really. For prosecutors like yourself, the gamble is winning the conviction and incarceration of people society looks down upon. People who are sacrificed by more sinister characters higher up a food chain. Or alternatively, being saddled with an ever-growing list of mortifying acquittals that could be your legacy. Sometimes the best and fairest hand you play is the one you fold early," said Eddie.

Eddie bid his old co-conspirator, Judge Hathaway, and the prissy Crown Prosecutor, Karen Mulgrave, adieu. He shook their hands and made his exit. In his once tasteful, rumpled old suit, Edward R. Novak slow-walked the corridors of justice out the door to his questionably obtained Rolls-Royce and drove his groceries home to his cabin by the lake.

Chapter 11

Try as he might, Eddie couldn't remember when he'd last filled his prescription. Months certainly, possibly a year. His Toronto doctor had explained the efficacy of 5-alpha reductase inhibitors to him and suggested he might benefit from consistent use. Eddie hadn't heeded his doctor's advice. Clearly, the episode with Rhonda and the resumption of spurting and dribbling were his cues to renew. With his now badly abraded nose, blackened eyes, and throbbing hamstring, Eddie stationed the Rolls well out of view of the Mercantile. He'd limp the distance from behind the pharmacy building to the front door if it meant avoiding being spotted by Rhonda.

Life in Cailly wasn't without social complexities. Having to dodge certain individuals could be difficult, whether it was the gloating winner of the annual Bake-Off, a contractor with whom one might have had unsatisfactory dealings, or of course, less likely but not unheard of, someone with whom one might have had an embarrassing intimate encounter. All part of the fabric of life in Cailly. Eddie gallantly stepped aside as several older women made their way out the pharmacy door. His happy anticipation of a chat with warm and cheerful Beth McIntyre was quickly dashed upon entry. Here he discovered Stephen Coutts and Matt Monwil in communion beside the stationary blood pressure cuff.

Instinctively calculating the terms of engagement, Eddie knew, when outnumbered, offence was required.

"Well. Wonders never cease. Mischief abounds. Good morning, gentlemen," said Eddie. Councillor Stephen Coutts and Bylaw Officer Matt Monwil now found themselves in the glaring headlights of Edward R. Novak. This was not Eddie's first encounter with Matthew Monwil. On more than one occasion, the two had shared happy recollection of their victory in the egg-and-spoon relay at the Cailly Regatta. The men had been paired for the race one year when Eddie still participated and Matt was still a teen.

"That's quite the look," said a visibly pleased Councillor Coutts, taking in the carnage of Eddie's now blackened eyes and swollen nose.

"Jeez, Eddie," said Bylaw Officer Monwil.

"And what pray tell brings you gentlemen here today?" Eddie asked.

Matt waved his white paper bag of medication. "Jen's got the gout."

"Sinus infection," said Stephen Coutts peevishly.

"Such afflictions," said Eddie.

"What brings you in?" Stephen further scrutinized Eddie's face.

"Live as long as I have, and you'll find out," Eddie warned.

"I'm probably further down that road than our friend Mattie here. He's still got young kids to look out for," said Councillor Coutts, cueing up Bylaw Officer Monwil.

Reading the tea leaves but still too green to understand how overmatched he was, Matt Monwil dutifully began the engagement Stephen Coutts seemed to be encouraging.

"Hey, Eddie, did you get the note I left you?" he asked without the vaguest seriousness.

"Note?" Eddie asked.

"Yeah, was out to your place the other day. Left a note on your door," Matt explained.

"Oh, did you?"

"Yeah, just to say, 'Call us,'" explained Matt.

"I'm sorry, I must have missed that."

"No problem. Anyway, yeah, so maybe you could call the office later," said Matt.

"Or maybe you could just tell me right now what your note was about," said Eddie.

Councillor Stephen Coutts stood, arms crossed, buckling up his front-row seat for the comeuppance he so hungrily wanted Eddie Novak to receive.

"Um, yeah, so I guess there were some trees taken down along the shoreline at your place, and uh, like, the Planning Act . . . You can't do that, eh?" Bylaw Officer Monwil informed him.

"Is that right?" asked Eddie.

"Yeah, so there's a fine and stuff." Matt gently bobbed his head. "The Planning Act says you can't take trees down on the shoreline."

With the curtain seeming to rise and the show apparently underway, a small smile creased Stephen Coutts's face as he began to roll back and forth from heel to toe. Eddie took it all in, standing in silent observation of the two.

"Fascinating. And so, Matthew, do tell, how was it you came to attend the property?" Eddie asked.

Matt swallowed visibly. "You know, uh, if you're takin' trees down, we come out and just, you know, make sure they're not anywhere near the shoreline."

"That's interesting," said Eddie, his brow furrowing in feigned confusion. "And how is it you'd come by this information that someone was taking trees down?"

"Well, I guess if we hear chainsaws or see the trees down or whatever, we come and take a look," said Matt.

"Right. And this is the way things are done?" inquired Eddie.

"Yeah," responded Matt.

"Now, just so I'm clear, the township enforces bylaws by monitoring and patrolling private property, before issuing fines. Is that what you're suggesting?" asked Eddie, presenting the upheld palm of his right hand.

"I wouldn't say *monitoring* or *patrolling* really. More like, if we get a complaint or whatever, then we'll go take a look."

As the words fell from Bylaw Officer Monwil's mouth, blood began to visibly drain from Stephen Coutts's face. Edward R. Novak LLB tingled. It was that one word. Eddie correctly read that Stephen Coutts knew this could be his undoing.

"Complaint?" Eddie asked with a smile.

"Or . . . whatever," Matt whispered under his breath.

"I should go," said Councillor Coutts.

"No. No, do stick around, Councillor. This is just getting interesting," said Eddie, placing his hand on Councillor Coutts's arm. "We're just getting started here, aren't we, Officer Monwil?"

"Anyway, yeah, there's a fine if you take trees down, and it looked like there were stumps there. Fresh stumps, so . . . I gotta put that in a report," said Matt.

"Oh, I see. A report," said Eddie.

"Yeah, a report," said Matt.

Eddie gently tightened his fingers around Councillor Coutts's forearm.

"You know, Officer Monwil, I really must compliment you on

your comprehensive grasp of the township's administrative policies," said Eddie.

"Huh?" said Matt.

"The township's bylaws are indeed complaint driven. You are correct. In fact, in order to proceed with a bylaw investigation or, in this case, property entry, a written complaint would have to be submitted to your office. Without putting too fine a point on it, the township actually requires the completion of a form for such complaints.

"Form?" inquired Councillor Coutts meekly.

"Yeah, there's a form," whispered Bylaw Officer Monwil.

"Now. In so far as you've apparently attended the property, I assume you're in possession of a completed Request for Service complaint form." Eddie leaned slightly toward Matt, his eyebrows raised. "Correct?"

"I . . . ah . . . I don't know, Eddie," Matt confessed.

"Well, you must know. I mean you'd have to. It's what the township requires."

"I really do need to run," said Councillor Coutts. Eddie retightened his grip on Stephen Coutts's arm, firmly restraining him from leaving.

"Noooo. No, I wouldn't hear of it, Steve. You need to stick around. I'm enjoying this. This little . . . *conflab*, this . . . this little gum-flap among old friends," said Eddie. "So, young Matthew, are you saying that you may not be in possession of a written Request for Service complaint form? Because I just want to be clear on all of this."

"I guess. Yeah, maybe, I dunno," said Matt, timorously.

"Well, look, that's no problem at all," said Eddie, grinning with enthusiasm.

"So . . . you're not mad or . . . ?" Matt asked, confused.

"Mad? Heavens no. Certainly not," said Eddie.

Councillor Coutts launched in. "Good 'cause it's just, people are takin' trees down all over, and you know, Matt's just doin' his job. Right?"

"Of course! Certainly!" Eddie laughed in agreement.

"Okay, so, what now?" asked Matt.

"Well, heck, fellas, there's a simple way to find out if there was a completed complaint form. It goes without saying you gents are familiar with the Freedom of Information Act, Part II, paragraph 10 (1). You know, the part where it says, 'Subject to subsections (1.1) and 69 (2), every person has a right of access to a record or a part of a record in the custody or under the control of an institution.' That's the part that allows me to make a request for a copy of the complaint form that Matt would have needed to access the property," said Eddie.

"But if there weren't a complaint form? Like, what would happen?" asked a now shaking Matt Monwil.

"Look, Matthew, I don't think there's any need to concern oneself about that. I'm sure the township would overlook a little thing like the absence of a simple form," said Eddie.

"Would they?" asked a now pale but hopeful Councillor Coutts.

"Sure, Steve, of course they would. I mean, provided the township had some other evidence of a complaint. You know, phone records, or emails, or text messages, that kind of thing. 'Course, all of that information could just as easily be asked for in a request for information under the Act. You know, all the stuff that would identify when the complaint was made and who made it. I think that would clear a lot of this up," said Eddie.

"Look, Eddie, we don't need to make a thing of this. I could just let the whole thing go," said Matt, frustrated and still shaking slightly.

Stephen began, "Matt's not trying to hass—"

"Sure, he is. Of course he is. That's exactly what he's trying to do," said Eddie.

Stephen Coutts tore his arm from Eddie's grip and squared his stance, making clear he wouldn't be contradicted this way. "Go ahead and ask, Eddie. Ask for whatever you like. What do you think is gonna happen?" he sneered.

"I guess we'll see. Won't we?" Eddie posited.

"I doubt it," said Stephen.

"Guys, I don't wanna get in the middle of whatever thing you got goin' on with each other. Leave me out of it," implored Matt.

"Leave you out of it? No, no, no young man. You're very much in it. And I have a pretty good idea who put you in it. I think we all know who that was, don't we?" asked Eddie.

"I reported it. Big deal. Nothing is gonna come of this, Matt. He's fulla shit," Stephen reassured him.

"Nothing? I'll give you this, you're confident. Misguided, but confident. Listen, Steve—"

"It's Stephen."

"Right. Sure. Let me give you boys a bit of insight. In my business, there's a few foundational rules, okay? One of them is this: Never threaten to do something you aren't fully prepared to do. So, when I tell you I'll make a request for information and run you both up the flagpole, believe me, I have the ability to do that, and fully intend to. And this brings me to your next sharp insight. About now, you're calculating the cost of this little contretemps, right? About now, you're asking yourself, 'So what? What if he does go down this road? What's gonna happen?' Let me stretch your understanding of this little game you boys are involved in, okay? You see, young Matthew, without a completed written complaint, you entered a property without proper authority. That's trespassing. As for you, Steve, well, what with you being the clever fellow that you are, of course you'd be familiar with section 140 (1) of the Criminal Code. You know, the part where it says, 'Every one commits public mischief who, with intent to mislead, causes a peace officer to enter on or continue an investigation by making a false statement that accuses some other person of having committed an offence . . .' You know, that part?" said Eddie.

"Owners are required to seek an allowance in a Planning Agreement, Eddie. You didn't do that," said Councillor Coutts.

"Aren't you clever, Steve. You're right. I didn't. Know why?" Eddie asked.

"No. I don't," confessed Stephen Coutts.

"Because I'm not the owner of that property. You made a false statement, Steve. That's a criminal code violation." Eddie let the words hang in the air as Stephen Coutts and Matt Monwil shifted uncomfortably on their feet. Defeated, Councillor Coutts attempted damage control with a conciliatory tone.

"Eddie, we don't need to . . ." Stephen began.

"Give it to him, Steve," said Eddie.

"What? Give who *what*?" asked Stephen, confused.

"Him," said Eddie, nodding his head toward Matt.

"I don't . . . I'm not sure I . . ." a bewildered-looking Stephen Coutts said.

"Come on, Steve. Don't pretend. You know very well what I'm talking about. What was it? What was the bargain? He must have wanted something? What was it?" Eddie pressed.

"I don't know what you're talking about," said Stephen.

"Sure, you do. Of course you do. You've got me curious. What was it? What was the thing you offered in exchange for giving me a problem about trees?" asked Eddie.

"Eddie, there's no problem here. I-I don't have to submit a report," stammered Matt.

"Behind-the-scenes quid pro quos. You know that's conspiracy, right? Matthew, tell me what you thought was of such value that you'd risk your job by trespassing on private property?" asked Eddie.

"Eddie, please, can we just . . ." Stephen begged.

"No, no, no. We're not done here. I'll tell you how we're going to settle this, okay?" asked Eddie.

"Okay, Eddie," said Stephen.

"Okay, Eddie," said Matt.

"Steve, you're going to tell Matt that you're going to give him what he wants. After I hear that, then you boys are going to go on your way. And Matthew, if you don't get what you want, you're going to come to me, and we can revisit all of this. Sound good?" Eddie proposed.

"All right, Eddie," said a now clearly frightened Stephen.

"Okay, sounds good, Eddie," said Matt.

"So can we go now?" asked Stephen.

"No. Not until I hear it. I want to hear you say it, Steve. I want to hear you tell Matt that you're going to get him, or give him, whatever the fuck it is he wants," said Eddie with evident menace.

"Matt, I'll get you your thing. The thing you wanted," whispered Councillor Coutts.

"No. No. No. You need to tell him exactly what it is you're going to get him, Steve. The thing. You need to say what the thing is," Eddie insisted.

Sighing and heaving his shoulders, Stephen Coutts said through pursed lips, "Fine. Matt, I'll get your place on the school bus route."

"Wonderful. There it is. Gents, I'm sure you both have busy

schedules," Eddie said, waving the two men off as he stepped forward to greet Beth. Shaken and agitated, Councillor Coutts and Bylaw Officer Monwil beat a quick and quiet retreat out the door.

Beth was as gracious and kind as she always was. Eddie completed his business with a caring admonition from Beth to stay on his medication if he wanted to enjoy a more comfortable day. She'd been extraordinarily helpful in recommending a pain-relieving ointment for a badly pulled muscle, and after a very pleasant chat, Eddie went for the exit. His sadistic persecution of his adversaries would not go unpunished however. Eddie's agonized collapse on top of Rhonda had apparently grievously aggravated her bad shoulder. En route to pick up her anti-inflammatory medication, Rhonda started with him as they passed in the doorway.

"Did you talk to 'em? Did you?" Rhonda barked.

"Good morning to you too, Rhonda," said Eddie.

"When will we hear?" Rhonda persisted.

"This is hardly the place or time to be discussing the matter. I'll come to the Mercantile in fifteen minutes," growled Eddie, hobbling past her out the door, then limping round to the back of the building.

Eddie drove to the liquor outlet. He couldn't face that woman stone-cold sober. And besides, it would be nice to speak with both Beth and her husband, Darren, within minutes of one another. Eddie was drawn to the McIntyres' decency and humanity. It was the respite and grounding he required, even if it was in the midst of seeking out the finest single malt Scotch whisky his local outlet carried. Uncharacteristically rattled by his go-round with the scheming Councillor Coutts and his guileless sidekick, Bylaw Officer Monwil, Eddie sat in the parking lot of the liquor outlet in his comfortable Rolls-Royce and calmed himself. It surprised him that after a lifetime of vicious litigation requiring the most cutthroat cunning, he could be as vexed as he was by all of this. His dismantling of their plot had been child's play, and yet here he sat, bothered, unsatisfied.

Eddie reclined his seat and watched the other alcoholics arrive at the outlet for their midmorning fix. There was a resigned honesty to all of it that touched him. By that hour most of the haggard folks arriving had abandoned any pretense of being anything other than what they were, and what they wanted. However sad it may have been, it was, if nothing else, honest.

The minutes ticked away as Eddie contemplated his impending meeting with Rhonda. How would he express his regret without further embarrassment to either of them? And then there was the task of explaining how his meeting with the judge and prosecutor might affect the outcome for young Travis. It would be difficult to explain how the wheels of justice worked, how relationships and personalities influenced the trajectory of a case. There was that obstacle and then the task of managing whatever unrealistic expectations she would certainly have. All of these things, and the pressing and perilous need for someone to contact Crown Prosecutor Karen Mulgrave.

An ancient banged-up green pickup pulled in three spots over. Eddie didn't know the driver's name but knew him by sight. His door opened slowly. Eddie watched as the old gent lifted his left leg out the door, hauled his right leg from the wheel well, and slid himself off the seat. Hanging onto the door before steadying his feet on the ground, the man began the shuffle of shame and desperation into the liquor outlet. Eddie gave close scrutiny to the bloodshot eyes, ruddy face, teetering steps, and the paradox of an emaciated frame with a distended belly. Where did he live? Did he have a wife? Children? Did he wake up alone?

Eddie took the keys from the ignition and stepped out of the Rolls. For a moment he stood watching the broken old soldier inside the liquor outlet counting change to pay for his bottle. He looked to the sky and watched grey autumn clouds roll overhead. He surveyed the river bridge, little Cailly Lake, and the fall colours against a darkening sky. As he moved to lock the door, Eddie caught his reflection in the window of the elegant Rolls-Royce Corniche. His bruised face; ragged suit; lifeless, thinning hair. Returning his gaze ever so briefly to the elderly gentleman, Eddie corrected his direction and began to limp in the direction of the Mercantile.

The jangly bell screen door announced Eddie's arrival. A couple of old dames from the Seniors' had made the walk over to pick up sundries. He watched as they opened their handbags to pay Rhonda and quietly stood aside as they passed on their way out.

"Did you talk to that Mulgrave lady?" Rhonda snarled. Blunt delivery was as natural to Rhonda as her mouth-breathing. Eddie welcomed the brevity if it meant avoidance of their embarrassing encounter.

"I did," said Eddie.

"Is he gonna go to jail?" Rhonda demanded.

"Rhonda, you don't just walk into a judge's chambers and make a sentencing deal. That's not how these things go," said Eddie.

"You lookin' for me to spread for you again?" barked Rhonda.

"No, madam, I am not. I spoke with the judge and the prosecutor. Travis should call her next week. If she asks where he was or why he didn't show up for pre-trial, he should tell her he was in Guelph for personal reasons and that he's not waiving anything until she puts something on the table. Travis should agree to summary mischief and nothing more. If she pushes the arson, negligence, possession, and production, he needs to talk to a lawyer right away," Eddie explained.

"He don't have no money for a lawyer. I told you that," said Rhonda.

"Yes, you've said that repeatedly. Travis could be gone for many, many years if the prosecutor runs with arson, negligence, and production," Eddie cautioned.

"He can't pay for no lawyer," Rhonda insisted.

"Well, so you say. Travis may have a problem on his hands then," said Eddie.

"He can't talk to no prosecutor. He barely got his grade eight." Rhonda appeared to stomp her right foot.

"Miss Lumley, my guess is, you're more than capable of stickhandling a third-year prosecutor. Call Miss Mulgrave yourself and put forward the position I've just laid out."

"You want me to talk to her?" asked Rhonda.

"I don't want anything. You want something. You're asking me for free legal advice. I'm giving it to you. Do as you please," said Eddie, growing frustrated. It was by now abundantly clear to Eddie that Rhonda was an ingrate and incapable of seeing others as anything more than an imposition or an opportunity. Leaving aside his own plotting in the face of Miss Mulgrave's largesse regarding his traffic violation, there were few things Edward R. Novak loathed more than ingratitude. Fortunately for Miss Lumley and her son, Travis Smith, prosecutors were on that brief list. Eddie would provide what guidance he could if it meant pulling a rug out from under a prosecutor.

"How am I supposed to know what to tell her?" Rhonda threw her hands in the air.

"I've just told you what needs to be communicated to the prosecutor," Eddie said with demonstrable indifference.

"But what if she starts askin' questions and tellin' me, no? I don't wanna talk to her," said Rhonda.

"Well then, I guess your son could be in considerable trouble," said Eddie.

"I never spoke to no prosecutor before."

Not wanting to extend the conversation further, Eddie cut to the quick. "Get a piece of paper and a pen."

She turned to the shelf behind her, took a pen and the torn envelope of a recent insurance bill, and placed them on the cabinet top in front of Eddie.

"I'm going to write down what you're going to say."

"I told you—"

"Stop talking," Eddie demanded. Pen in hand, he carefully considered what was needed. Brevity was required. Simplicity and a nonconfrontational tone were required. There on the back of an old envelope, Eddie began writing what might govern the outcome of young Travis Smith's life. Misgivings about Rhonda's rhetorical deficiencies were quickly discarded. He'd gamble on the connecting tissue of his carefully staged proxy arguments and Rhonda's capacity for self-interested compromise. Given the impressive daring of having offered a sexual liaison, a gambit Rhonda correctly calculated would be advantageous, Eddie bet on her ability to find just the right note with Karen Mulgrave.

Eddie laid the pen down. He stepped back and silently read his creation. Rhonda waited impatiently.

"I'm supposed to tell her all that?" Rhonda asked.

"Yes. You're going to read this very carefully. You're going to practise saying it out loud," Eddie advised.

"How many fuckin' times I gotta tell you? I don't wanna talk to her," Rhonda barked.

"You're not going to," said Eddie.

"Huh?" said Rhonda.

"You're going to call her office in the evening. After she's gone. You'll get her voice mail. You're going to leave a message. What I've written here is the message you're going to leave. Read this exactly as it's written. Don't add anything and don't leave anything out," Eddie instructed.

Rhonda took the envelope from him and began to silently read. Eddie watched until her lips stopped moving.

"Is there anything you don't understand?" he asked.

"You think this is gonna help?" asked Rhonda.

"There's no way of knowing that. Now read it to me."

"Out loud?" asked Rhonda.

With a heavy sigh of frustration and disbelief, Eddie confirmed, "Yes. Out loud."

Rhonda took a deep breath and nervously began. "'Hello, Miss Mulgrave, my name is Rhonda Lumley. I'm Travis Smith's mom. Travis is very sorry he couldn't come to the pre-trial. He's trying to get better and wanted to come but couldn't make it. He asked me to call you and tell you he knows he needs to appear in court. Travis knows he did wrong things but never wanted to hurt anyone. He has a lot of problems from his childhood. I hope you can help my Travis, Miss Mulgrave. He's a mixed-up kid, but I count on him for so much. I'm older now and having a hard time. I can't do a lot of the things I used to. Travis does most of the chores. He's all I have. Please, please, help my Travis, Miss Mulgrave. Thank you.' I'm supposed to say all this to her? Travis don't do no chores. He never done nothin' for me," said Rhonda.

"Rhonda, you asked for my help. This is what the help looks like. I'm not going to debate the matter with you," said Eddie.

"So, I should call her and read this into her voice mail?"

"Yes, that's what you should do. Practise it as many times as you can before you call. You don't want to sound like you're reading it," said Eddie.

"Will it keep him outta jail?" asked Rhonda.

"There's no guarantee he won't be incarcerated. He's facing serious charges and doesn't have a lawyer. This is not the best way to keep your son out of jail," cautioned Eddie.

"Did you take cigarettes outta my cabinet?" Rhonda asked accusingly.

"I beg your pardon?" said Eddie, indignant.

"I did inventory yesterday. Four packs are missing," said Rhonda.

"I have no idea what you're talking about," said Eddie.

"Travis says you was in here alone," Rhonda explained.

"Allegedly missing cigarettes should be the least of your concerns. You'd be well advised to focus on finding a criminal defence lawyer and keeping Travis out of jail," Eddie snarled, turning on his heel, and limping out the jangly bell screen door.

Eddie hobbled along back to the liquor outlet. How had he found himself in the middle of these messes? As incidental as these petty conflicts might have been at an earlier time in his life, he no longer had the energy to intimidate, humiliate, and decimate his adversaries. He no longer relished a fight. All the things he'd relied on so consistently in his life no longer came as effortlessly as they once had. The hobbling was irritating his inflamed hamstring. Eddie needed to sit. He shook his head and smiled through the pain as he made his way back to the Rolls. Of all of the grotesqueries, in all of the locations and circumstances, with all of the women he'd experienced along the way, serious self-injury had to be one of his more undignified disasters. The absurdity of it amused him.

More of the regulars had arrived at the liquor outlet by the time Eddie returned to the Rolls. A cigarette was needed. Eddie leaned against his ride, smoking and watching as the usuals ducked in and out, caching their solace in brown paper bags. A simple trip to the pharmacy had become a minefield of aggravation. In pain and now irritated, Eddie wanted nothing more than to be seated on his shoreline. He wanted to look at his lake, and the fall colours, and the granite cliffs that for so many years had brought him calm. Eddie butted his cigarette on the parking lot ground, opened the door to his sumptuous 1972 Rolls-Royce Corniche convertible, and began his journey home.

The golds and reds and oranges of autumn settled him. Savouring every river and crest of every hill, Eddie drove slowly back to his sanctuary. Perfect circumstances for Mahler. *Kindertotenlieder*, he thought. Eddie hummed and sang to fortify himself for the impending trek through the bush. With his hamstring now throbbing, his stamina would be tested. There were hazards all along the trail. Unstable terrain, mud, wild animals, obstacles of all sorts stood between Eddie and his refuge. As his destination drew nearer, he pondered how he'd come to conflict with Stephen Coutts, how he'd become embroiled with Rhonda and Travis.

Yes, certainly Eddie felt Matthew Monwil's visit and insipid note were an intrusion, but had he himself not precipitated the conflict with Stephen Coutts? Surely, Councillor Coutts was overreaching with his nosy and ill-informed commentary about bylaws, but had Eddie himself not been unnecessarily rude and gratuitously demeaning to the councillor? Had he not miscalculated the cost of his own brutally blunt and defensive hostility?

Eddie stowed the Rolls in his drive shed, locked it, and began a slow and agonized hike through the forest. Sharp, shooting pains in his hamstring wearied him. As restorative as the trail had been over the decades, he considered the benefits of rapid access to the outside world from his winter accommodation at the Blu-Jay Motel. Ease of access to newspapers, telephones, and groceries was among the small consolations of being stuck in town for the winter. He tired of having to drive to town, home from town, and carry groceries back through the narrow forest trail.

Eddie made a slow ascent up the steep final hill before the trail ran down to his cabin. The smooth outcropping of pink granite cresting above the treetops was Eddie's favourite spot along the trail. Its rounded summit matched the elevation of the cliffs he could see across the lake. Today he'd sit and rest. His aching leg had left him exhausted and on edge. Eddie took in the horizon in all directions and the circus of autumn colour under the sun at noon on an early October day. He lowered himself slowly and sat. The sun-warmed rock soothed his aching hamstring. He reclined and let the warmth soak into his resting body. High white clouds drifted across the sky as a cool breeze gently caressed his bristled and broken face.

From his back, Eddie watched a turkey vulture overhead. He admired its efficiency as it circled motionlessly on rising air. It called to mind some piece by Schubert, the name of which he couldn't quite retrieve. Eddie rested and let the notes play in his head. The name would come to him eventually. The sun moved from twelve o'clock to one before Eddie sat up. He was in no hurry to leave this spot. He drank it in just as he had for more than seventy years. He absorbed the expanse that stretched out beyond him. The endless banquet of trees, glittering water, limitless sky, all of it. Eddie was no more than three years old when he saw an eagle for the first time from here. He'd seen many birds since: falcons, merlins, eagles, hawks, osprey. From his earliest days he'd scaled this hill to watch them hunt. He'd watched cackling crows alighting on trees, woodpeckers pecking for ants, starlings harvesting grubs.

Over many years he'd met both friend and foe along the trail. He'd been fascinated by all of it: moose, bear, deer, coyote, wolf, skunk, mink, marten, raccoon, rabbit, even the tiniest mouse and shrew. He'd read books about all of these animals, the things they ate, and how they lived. He'd studied entomology textbooks to learn about the insects that fed on leaves, and bark, and carrion. He knew their Latin names and where they hid.

Below the lowering arc of autumn sun, Eddie finally eased his way down to the cabin and lake. Cooler air swept round his ankles. He built a fire and sat on a cut log stump. By the warmth of the fire, he watched the afternoon light dappling the ground beneath the trees. The hours passed. The lake settled into stillness. He drank in the scent of smoke and an ancient white pine at the edge of his clearing. He listened as a jar of nuthatches chittered in the scrub. This place had served him well. Its fish, and game, and splendour had fed him.

Eddie cooked pickerel and a sweet potato on his fire, ate, and sat until twilight. As a near-full moon rose on the east side of the lake, he closed the cabin door for the night. A cold October dampness hung inside the cabin. Eddie lit a fire in the wood stove. From his porch shelf, he took a candle and placed it by his bed. Its flame would take the edge off the dampness before the wood stove fully warmed the building. He took woollen blankets from a closet and laid them over his bed. He doffed his suit coat, left his stained old dress shirt on, and pulled a ratty sweater over his head. He skipped the comfort of his customary nighttime tipple, kicked off his shoes, and retreated under the covers of his bed.

Eddie lay awake searching for the name of that piece stuck in his head. He'd hummed it all afternoon. It was one of Schubert's lieds, of course, he knew that much. But which one? Did his daughter share his love of music? He thought of that afternoon, watching her little-girl arms tapping an overturned pot on the cabin floor, just steps from where he now lay. Did she remember this place? Him? He recalled the letters he'd written her, reciting them word for word in his mind. Some unknown angst came then. Was there a more precise word, a simpler turn of phrase, he could have used? What was he trying to achieve by conveying sorrow and regret for his absence? Had his words failed him with Melanie? Had he misjudged his approach in the same way he'd misjudged his belligerent and unnecessary response to Stephen Coutts's inquiries about taking trees down? These misgivings troubled him.

Any regret Eddie felt about telling Stephen Coutts to fuck off was mitigated, however, in view of the councillor's cynical abuse of elected office. The brutal lesson Edward R. Novak had administered was well deserved in this case. While his profane response to Stephen's original inquiry surely precipitated the scheming, his adversary had overreached and suffered the consequences. Such was not the case with his daughter. The circumstances were different. Melanie was not his adversary. She was collateral damage in the wreckage of Eddie's life. He didn't know Melanie and had no way of assessing what weight, if any, his words might have with her.

Edward R. Novak's tools had grown dull. The fine balance of his despicable vices and his ability to extricate himself from their outcomes had tipped decidedly in the direction of failure.

Eddie lay thinking; what was it about Annabel's letter that had so inspired his anger? Something. She'd expressed herself in a way that chafed. She'd used words in a way that ignored the unspoken rules of their communication.

She'd described his "high rhetoric" and referenced previous conversations about his lifestyle and behaviour as "hardly useful." He considered her words, her phrasing, and syntax. The subtle intent was there. It seemed obvious to him now. In this instance, "high rhetoric" did not mean *erudite* or *articulate*. The sarcasm had escaped him on initial reading. The discarding of their prior interchanges concerning his lifestyle and behaviour as "hardly useful" was in fact a dismissal of anything he'd said on the topic. Eddie curled himself into a tight ball under the covers. Annabel had been telling him he was full of shit.

Eddie snuffed the bedside candle. Beneath a cold and cloudless October sky, moonlight cast shadows across his blankets. Eddie's stock was trading low. By what right was he reaching out to his daughter now, after forty years? Eddie saw the inanity of it. It wasn't what he'd written to Melanie; it was the emptiness of his words.

How would he fix this? It seemed his instinct to correct the first letter with another might have been grossly miscalculated. Even if his letters were intended to promote trust, this was not a problem solved with words. There in the solitary quiet of a bracing autumn night, the picture came clearer for Eddie Novak. Once the ornate bricks of a castle, his words had become an anvil tied to his ankle. Who was Edward R. Novak to have sent his daughter a single letter, never mind two? Where had he been throughout her life? What had he done? How could mere words mean anything to Melanie? Action was required. He would go to her. He would fly to Wyoming and meet his daughter, face to face.

Chapter 12

Eddie had no way of knowing when he'd return from his trip to Wyoming. It could be a day, a week, a month. The cabin would have to be packed up and secured for the season. He wouldn't risk trying to do all of that in the middle of November. Even a small blanketing of snow could greatly complicate matters. The pack-up was no easy feat. Most years it was two, often three days of toing and froing to prepare the cabin and property for winter. Eddie would need to eat or toss all of his food, which meant hauling garbage to the firepit or the dump. He'd drag out the plywood window covers he kept tucked under the building and install them on the soon-to-be-vacated cabin. An unoccupied cabin meant the arrival of mice, so he'd set out the traps and poison. He'd drag the canoe up near the cabin and stow the paddles under it. And then of course, he'd pack up his clothes and books and sundries and hump all the loads along the trail to the Rolls. And still the work wouldn't be done. He had logs to chop and stack for spring, and he'd cover the woodpile against snow and rain. The list of tasks was long. There was work to be done before arranging travel.

It was not Eddie's ordinary pack-up. He'd always taken a slow approach to seasonal shutdown. This year, Eddie was possessed of purpose and resolve. He could see and feel that his decades-long cycle of yearning, hesitation, inaction, self-soothing, and regret would shortly be behind him. He didn't know what lay on the other side of his decision to seek and find his daughter. He knew, however, that whatever might come, it could not possibly be worse than living the rest of his days without ever seeing her, knowing her, telling her in person, he was sorry.

As Eddie went about his business with new-found purpose, he ruminated on the path his life had taken. Stowing his canoe, paddles, and fishing rods, gathering and storing his tools, and boxing his things, Eddie considered the possibility of total rejection. It was weeks since his first letter to Melanie, and he'd received nothing in response. When he pondered his perverse life and the abandonment of his child, the shame and sadness broke him. Melanie had every right to ignore his entreaties. On what basis would she trust him? Certainly, if the Garland family had anything to say about him, it would not be pleasant. Nor would the internet yield encouraging information.

The dull ache in Eddie's hamstring seemed to be improving. Still, it was sore, and he was careful not to cause unnecessary strain, bending and lifting with considerable caution. He needed to conserve energy for the necessary trips back and forth along the trail over the next couple of days. Eddie never ceased to wonder at the volume of clutter he accumulated over the spring and summer months. What could stay, and what must go? How much could he carry across the trail at once? How many trips would be required? What could he store and what would he bring to the Blu-Jay Motel? All these questions.

Sectioned logs from trees Eddie had taken down weeks ago lay here and there. After several hours of organizing items in and around the cabin, Eddie spent the remainder of the morning chopping and stacking wood for the spring. After stacking the final piece, he tottered back to the cabin, exhausted. He sat for a moment and surveyed the boxes and bags he'd left around. The activity and disarray upended him. He could use a drink. Eddie pushed away the notion as quickly as it arrived. He needed to rest. Eddie made his way into his little cabin bedroom to lie down. He'd make a trip to the dump this afternoon after his nap. Tomorrow, he'd drive to his storage locker in Gravenhurst and drop items off. On his way home, he'd stop in Huntsville at the Blu-Jay and leave items there. He'd return for his final night at the cabin and leave the next day for Casper.

Eddie awoke from his snooze to dampness on his thigh. He'd been asleep long enough that any warmth from the urine he'd dribbled had cooled and woken him. He looked quickly to the window to see what afternoon light remained. He'd have to hurry if he wanted to make the dump. Eddie quickly went about gathering the items he'd set aside for the dump. He placed them in the centre of an old drop cloth, folded the corners in, and tied it. He closed the door to the cabin and threw the drop cloth over his shoulder before beginning the trek.

As much as he might have wanted to rest atop the granite summit of the hill that ran down to the cabin, he had no more than two hours of sun left. The trail hike would take close to an hour of that. The ten or so kilometres to the dump and back to the drive shed was typically a half hour. At best he'd finish the trek home fighting the dark. Eddie moved with as much haste and dispatch as he could muster. Carrying a heavy sack of garbage was not helping his cause. With his hands clasping the drop cloth slung over his shoulder, Eddie had no way of steadying himself or pushing back the branches slapping at his still-blackened eyes and bruised nose. He staggered on, finally reaching the drive shed.

The dumpsite was busier than usual. Eddie greeted Tim at the gate. After pleasantries and a quick look in the trunk, Tim waved him on. Eddie was careful to steer away from areas where pickup trucks were dumping. On two separate occasions he'd had the misfortune of punctured tires; in both instances, drywall screws dropped from construction trucks. Garbage tossed, Eddie spun for the exit and pulled back onto the concession road for the trip back. It felt good to shed his clutter and waste. Eddie lowered the windows to feel the cool wind on his beaten-up face. The ramshackle hobby farms along the way, with their stony fields, scraggly animals, and patchwork fencing felt more forlorn under thick grey clouds. This was not farm country. It had never been farm country. The innocence of such endeavours charmed Eddie.

The Rolls rounded the corner onto the dirt road leading to the drive shed and trail. Despite diminishing light, Eddie took his time. He was keenly aware of the punishing rocks that, with a misplaced wheel and a little too much speed, could take out a ball joint or muffler. After parking the Rolls and locking the drive shed door, Eddie began the trek through the bush to his cabin. Another night, another day, and another night after that, and he'd leave for Casper, Wyoming. He'd confront his darkest fear, suffer his deepest shame. He'd look his daughter in the eye and accept responsibility for his most colossal failure.

Darkening clouds over a fading sun made Eddie's trail hike more difficult. He hurried to the extent his sore leg would allow. Loath as he might have been to admit it, the steep inclines and declines, branch intrusions, rocks, and roots held less pleasure for Eddie these days. Well-aged oxford loafers certainly didn't help. The Schubert piece returned to him as he inched his way down one of the trickier slopes. Eddie hummed its melody in hope of recalling the name, the sweet and musky scent of autumn decay filling his lungs.

Eddie arrived at the summit of the granite outcropping. With the sun dipping behind him in the west, he stopped for a moment and scanned the nearly dark eastern horizon. What a wonder. What a gift this place had been to him. Standing silent, Eddie listened and rested in equanimity as day creatures found beds and night creatures roused. He contemplated the beautiful ruggedness of this place: the forest, the animals, the rocks, and the waterways. None of them cared about Eddie's troubles or pleasures. Eddie had been alone here long enough now. It was time to share the wonder of this place. To share it with someone he hoped would care for his troubles and pleasures.

With little light left in the evening sky, Eddie began the descent to the cabin. He stepped gingerly toward the flattening edge of the outcropping where thin soil met rock. He oriented himself by taking the brush on the left and right in his hands before entering the dark earth trail down to the cabin. Easing ahead slowly, Eddie resumed his full-throated humming of the Schubert piece he still couldn't name. Step by step, sideways at times, Eddie drew nearer to the cabin. He'd make himself a hot pot of ginseng tea. That would be the perfect end to his day. No sooner than finishing the thought, the toe of his right shoe caught a thick root. He stumbled forward, narrowly regaining his footing. Jarred from thoughts of hot tea and slightly off kilter by the stumble, Eddie then misjudged a rock in the dark. Without the depth perception afforded by better light, he underestimated a sharply angled surface, seeing the rock as flatter than its actual incline. His ankle rolled, sending him sprawling down and sideways into dense undergrowth, and his head struck some unseen thing.

Eddie's ankle stung. His oxford and sock seemed to tighten

instantly. Choosing to gather his wits rather than make an attempt to stand, Eddie lay motionless on his left side in the growing dark, his face resting an inch from the dirt. A wet warmth gathered round his right temple. Eddie took a mental inventory. What hurt? What didn't? Where was he situated on the hill? How much farther did he have to go? The smell of soil and rotting leaves filled his nostrils. No more than a minute passed. Eddie groaned from the pain in his ankle. He rolled onto his stomach and pushed himself up on all fours, gathered himself a moment, and crawled back up onto the trail.

He stood up, careful not to rest on his turned foot. He shifted his weight and tested the pain. Certainly uncomfortable, but not excruciating. Not so painful he wouldn't be able to bear some weight. Only when he began to lurch forward did the fullness of his circumstances come to the fore. His left hamstring was still very tender, and now his right ankle had become unstable. Eddie sat down in the middle of the trail. Walking upright wouldn't work. He'd need another way home. Eddie lay back a moment to think. The denseness of forest and thickness of cloud left him in utter darkness. Now was as good a time as any for a cigarette. He lit a cigarette pulled from the pack of du Mauriers in his suit coat pocket. If he couldn't move, at least he'd enjoy a smoke in peace and quiet.

Eddie rested, and smoked, and thought of Schubert. It nagged away at him. One of those things. It was right there, just on the tip of his tongue. A quartet. D minor, he thought. A faint itch caught Eddie's cheek. He scratched and felt something on his face. He brought the light of his cigarette to his hand. Drying blood. He ran his hand up the side of his head. His fingertips traced a rise from his temple across his forehead. Eddie knew on instinct this was a deep cut. It occurred to him that the scent of his blood might attract attention he didn't want. He finished his cigarette, rolled onto his knees, and began a careful crawl down the rocky earth to his cabin.

Nearing the bottom of the hill, Eddie pushed himself up onto his feet. His sock was stretched tight across a now-bulging ankle. The pain was bad but not as bad as he'd feared. Grateful not to have broken his ankle, Eddie gently hobbled to his door and entered. Tomorrow would be a challenge. With a sore hamstring, a twisted ankle, a bruised nose, blackened eyes, and now a serious cut on his forehead, Eddie had seen better days. He still needed to haul a variety of items over the trail to his car, deliver his items to the storage locker in Gravenhurst, drop his clothes off at the Blu-Jay Motel, gas up the Rolls-Royce Corniche for a trip to the airport, and get back to the cabin for his final night. Eddie collapsed into his recliner to rest. He lay back and let Schubert fill his head. Night drew down, and sleep overtook him.

The hours passed. The night temperature dropped. Eddie awoke, shaking with cold. He opened his eyes to a dark cabin. His ankle throbbed. He fumbled his way out of the recliner and over to the little wood stove. From his knees, Eddie loaded the stove with paper and bits of kindling. He lit the fire and inched to the wooden countertop. Grabbing a tea towel and a flashlight, he eased his way down the stairs. Slowly, following the light, he made his way to the lake, where he lowered himself and sat on the shoreline. His hamstring twinging, his ankle throbbing, Eddie removed his loafer and sock. He probed the thickness of his ankle briefly, then lowered his foot into the cold water. The water made his foot prickle but brought relief to his aching ankle. Eddie sat as long as he could, shivering in the cold October night.

When the cold finally got the better of him, Eddie plunged the tea towel into the water, pulled it out, twisted the water from it, wiped blood from his face and head, and wrapped his ankle before straggling back to the cabin by the light of his flashlight. The kindling had done little to warm the building just yet. He placed a small log on the flames, poured water from his jug into the kettle, and laid the kettle on the wood stove. He put a tiny sachet of ginseng tea in a cup. Eddie sat in his recliner to wait out the boiling. As the fire rose, the cold slowly abated, but it was several minutes before he stopped shivering.

Eddie wanted a drink from his remaining bottle of single malt. He longed for the relief. He sipped tea instead. It might have been one or two o'clock in the morning. He had no idea. The cabin warmed enough for Eddie to sleep. He'd raised his body temperature with the tea, and he was ready for deep rest.

Eddie struggled to his bed, pulled his coat and pants from his body, and slipped under the covers. His body ached. The cut on his forehead stung; his ankle and hamstring throbbed. The ribs he'd landed on, now tender when he breathed. He plunged into dreamless sleep for many hours.

It was midmorning before Eddie awoke. The height of the sun took him by surprise. He hadn't intended to sleep this late. Rolling from his bed, Eddie moved his foot slightly to test his ankle. Swelling had subsided overnight, and though still tender, the pain was no longer intense. He wasted no time as he went about his morning ritual: dressing, brushing teeth, a cup of tea, a crisp fall apple, a crust of bread with jam. Eddie had burned precious daylight when there was work to do.

With his clothes packed into a large duffle bag, Eddie moved on to cleaning up and storing his tools. A small plastic bin he loaded with a handful of books, a few perishables from his little bar fridge, shotgun cartridges, a half pack of cigarettes found under his bed, odds and sods. He checked the barrel of his shotgun and put the safety on before placing the firearm in its carrying bag. The work was slow. Eddie's body cried out for rest at every turn. He'd prided himself on his agility and nimble movement over the years. Today was not one of those days. Today he saw himself alone and moving in ways he imagined elderly people moved.

It was several hours before Eddie was ready to go. On a good day this would be a difficult trek along the trail. With a duffle bag over his shoulder, the bin of sundries in his hands, and the shotgun slung across his back, Eddie's twisted ankle and tight hamstring made it all the more difficult. Hauling his things out at the end of the season was always a dreaded task. All of it fraught with anxiety about how his little cabin would fare over the winter with its ferocious blizzards. Eddie didn't like having to leave the lake this time of year. He didn't like having to carry clothing and accoutrements on a forty-five-minute hike through the bush. It was usually cold; he often dropped things and had to stop to pick up and reorganize. Today he'd be lucky to make it to the Rolls at all.

The hike was plodding. Eddie wouldn't risk another tumble. Even if he'd wanted to hurry, he couldn't. He wasn't eight hundred metres up the trail before his ankle began to throb. He began calculating his rest stop. He'd already passed the granite outcropping. The little clearing just down the way from the outcropping might do but was still too close to the cabin. It didn't make sense to stop there. There was a gully about halfway that could work. Not much in the way of places to lie down, but it would do. He'd make a spot.

Eddie laboriously humped his way along, careful not to topple over. The idea of a sexual liaison resulting in a badly pulled muscle and facial injuries followed by a pratfall down a muddy hill in the darkness . . . it was all very discouraging. Still, there was the saving grace of being far away from Toronto, where he'd practised law for fifty years—forty-six years and eight months, accounting for periods of suspension. Eddie was grateful for the distance, feeling spared the public indignity of age-related physical infirmity. He smiled in reflection on a life he could no longer fully recognize. He'd never been all that bothered by things others might be bothered by. Year after year, decade after decade, Edward R. Novak had marched into courtrooms completely unabashed by his many clashes with the Law Society, newspaper and television coverage of his many outrages, the scorn and ridicule of his colleagues, his creditors' loathing, the fury of many women. None of it had mattered much to Eddie. In fact, Eddie had enjoyed his role as wolfish belligerent. To be cast in the part of staggering fawn, however, he could not abide.

After a gentle descent to the little gully, Eddie took a seat on a log, resting his wonky ankle atop the bin of sundries. Eddie looked skyward and watched the dark-grey clouds rolling in. It would rain shortly. The Schubert piece rose up, and Eddie began to hum its finale.

Eddie took inventory of his clutter. Stinking clothing, rags really; his cigarettes; other things; a shotgun and some shells. What was the meaning or use for any of it now? A grave darkness filled him. One more night. One single night to spend before flying to a place where he hoped the darkness would be lifted from him.

Trudging slowly once again through the bush, Eddie carried on the rest of the way, reaching the drive shed only moments before the sky opened in a downpour of cold October rain. After a quick rest on the rear bumper of the Rolls, he carefully climbed the ladder inside the drive shed to the plywood loft. He retrieved the metal lockbox, climbed down, and placed it on the back seat of the Rolls. After loading his gear into the trunk, Eddie got on his way. He wasn't yet to the concession road before the pounding rain eased to a morose drizzle. The drizzle shortly gave way to a drifting autumn mist and a cool dampness that hung in the air.

Eddie took in the spectacular autumn colours as he cruised down the big highway. Sparkling wet leaves were a pleasant distraction from the pain. Eddie cut a sorry figure. There was, however, the exquisite comfort of the Rolls-Royce Corniche and the pleasing sight of flocks of coloured leaves scattering the sky on autumn winds.

On arrival at the Gravenhurst Hidey-Hole Storage Rental, Eddie spun the Rolls around and reversed toward the concrete dock at his locker. After a slow and wary step out of the Rolls, Eddie found the locker key on his keyring. Eddie would need to find a place for his sundries, his shotgun, and his lockbox of cash. There might have been more room in the cluttered storage space had Eddie bothered to organize his things. As it was, the space was near impassable with a leather couch, silver tea service, wingback chairs, bookshelves, a Tiffany lamp, washer and dryer, side tables, an old upright piano, paintings, an office desk, dining room table and chairs, boxes of kitchen utensils, pots and pans, stacks of fine dishware, piles of moth-eaten tailored suits, a bin filled with Italian leather loafers, and boxes of unknown content, placed indiscriminately here and there. All of it useless to him now.

A quick scan of the parking area found no onlookers. Eddie retrieved his shotgun from the trunk and laid it across the seats of the leather couch in the middle of the space. He set his plastic bin amidst a cluster of cardboard boxes. To stow his metal cashbox, he climbed as best he could over the furnishings and clutter to the deepest corner of the locker. He pulled back a handful of old sheets heaped there. He opened the cashbox, removed and pocketed a thick stack of fifty- and hundred-dollar bills. After relocking the cashbox, Eddie placed it on top of a dozen other stuffed cashboxes, then returned the sheets to cover the loot.

He dumped unfolded shirts from a carry-on travel case retrieved from under his old dining room table. Then pulled sweaters, socks, and underwear from a row of bulging green garbage bags lining the wall of the locker. He stuffed the items into the travel case and retrieved one of his old winter suits and a trench coat, slung them over his arm, and exited the locker with his carry-on suitcase. Eddie locked up, piled his things on the back seat of the Rolls, and began the trip back to Huntsville. Save for a handful of minor items he still needed to retrieve from the cabin, Eddie had all but fully executed the seasonal closing.

The Blu-Jay Motel seemed unusually active. There were at least three other vehicles in the parking lot when Eddie pulled in. He braced himself for what he anticipated would be a painful conversation with Taylor. Eddie needed to explain to her that he simply required a place to store his duffle bag, some toiletries, and two or three books he was reading. He'd need to tell her that although he was checking in, he wouldn't be staying this evening. Eddie was confident that the complexity of checking in, not staying immediately, but returning the next day, would cause synaptic chaos for young Taylor.

A wave of relief swept over him as he passed through the doorway. Mrs. Papadopoulos sat calmly and quietly behind the desk. Eddie would need to express compassion and condolences, sympathy and concern. This seemed a far easier task than the patience required for a conversation with Taylor. He'd learned over many years that sometimes the best expression in these situations was no expression. A simple nod and concerned look often worked. In some cases, a perfunctory condolence cliché could create the verisimilitude of compassion he was looking for.

Eddie extended his hand across the desk to Helen. "Hello, Mrs. Papadopoulos. I'm so terribly sorry to hear of Gus's passing. What a tragedy," said Eddie, allowing her to hold his hand far longer than he'd expected she might. After condolences, pleasantries, and brief reminiscences, sorrowful Helen provided the key to what would become Eddie's winter home.

Eddie exited the front office area and hobbled along the cracked concrete walkway to room 3. He left the door ajar and plunked down on the bed. Eddie savoured the mundanity of this place. There was comfort within the Blu-Jay's unremarkable fixtures and walls. He was anonymous here. He could be any traveller. He rested momentarily and thought about what it would be like to look into his daughter's eyes for the first time in forty-one years. What would her voice sound like? Presuming she didn't simply shut a door in his face without speaking. It was all a risk. One he must take. Soon, he moved the Rolls over to the parking spot in front of room 3. He took his time unloading. After making his nest, Eddie checked his pilfered retirement watch. The timing was perfect. If he left presently, he'd arrive in Cailly when he needed to.

The big highway north was near empty this fall afternoon. Ideal for silent contemplation. If things worked to plan, Travis would walk. By all rights he should spend time behind bars, Eddie knew this of course. Travis just needed time before any deal could be made. The trick was to have bought him enough runway before the real fish was caught.

Eddie drove the big highway north from Huntsville up to the Emsdale county road. He slowed, rounding the curve down the off-ramp. A Provincial Police cruiser sat on the right shoulder, thirty metres east along the county road. The officers would certainly know Eddie's Rolls-Royce Corniche on sight. Eddie crept by, slowing to turn his head their way. He exchanged nods and faint smiles with the two uniformed officers. To the extent his tender ankle would allow, Eddie gently pressed on the accelerator. The trees, the hills and valleys, creeks and streams seemed to intensify in their beauty now. Battered face and body aside, Eddie felt more alive than he had in many months.

The intersecting concession road north to Rhonda's loomed just up ahead. Eddie slowed enough through the crossroads to note the parked police cruiser just within eyesight well south of the intersection. He smiled and resumed his pace toward Cailly. A strong wind began to blow. The trees along the county road shook leaves from their branches in great showers of colour. It was all so lovely. Today was going to be a good day.

The sleepy off-season tempo had set in. Cailly was predictably quiet. A handful of folks going about their business; locals in town to pay their taxes, pick up prescriptions or a bottle. As Eddie's chariot ferried him over the river bridge, he spied yet another police cruiser tucked in beside the township office. Edward R. Novak marvelled at the failure of discretion. He cruised up the main drag, pulled into Merv's, and stopped in front of the primitive gas pump. He lowered his window, turned the car off, and waited a moment before Merv ambled out of the service bay.

"I won't ask what mischief has put your face off. Not lookin' good, whatever it was," said Merv.

"Oh, Mervin, you've no idea," said Eddie, shaking his head.

"Don't let Darren see you like that. You'll never hear the end of it."

"I'm aware," said Eddie.

"Saw you when you went through earlier. Thought you were gonna gas up," said Merv.

"Had enough to get me to Gravenhurst and back. Please fill it, Merv. I'm off early tomorrow. Not sure when I'll be back," said Eddie as he laboured out of the Rolls.

"Where ya headed, son?" Merv inquired, placing the nozzle into the tank.

"That's a long story," said Eddie. He paused a moment, took a deep breath, summoned his courage, and let the words fall from his lips. "The short story is, I'm headed out west to see my daughter." Eddie walked slowly round to the other side of the Rolls, watching carefully as Merv's eyes widened and his jaw went slack.

"Your what?"

"My daughter."

"Your daughter?"

"Yes, my daughter." Eddie wasn't sure how to interpret the silence that followed. In the many decades Eddie had known Merv, never once had he mentioned a daughter. There were rare occasions when Eddie had referenced a wife, but never, ever, a daughter. Merv might have supposed that Eddie didn't have children, and if he had, it was because Eddie had never even hinted at having children. It scarcely mattered whether it was assumption on Merv's part, concealment on Eddie's part, or that the subject had just never come up; a bomb had been dropped. Merv visibly reeled.

With a few gentle pumps of the lever, Merv topped up the tank. Eddie stood scanning the road down to the township office. He quickly turned to Merv and placed his hand on Merv's wrist. "Leave it," said Eddie.

"What?" asked Merv.

"Leave it," Eddie instructed, nodding toward the stopped nozzle Merv was about to retract. "Leave it where it is."

"What are you on about there, fella?" asked Merv.

"Leave it in the tank. Watch. We're just having a conversation, all right? Look at me. Okay? We're just having a conversation like we always do." Eddie released Merv's wrist as Merv complied.

"Are you all right today, Eddie?"

"Don't move. Just talk. We're just talking here," said Eddie, quietly holding his gaze on Merv. No more than twelve seconds passed when the sirens started. Three Provincial Police cruisers flew into town and descended on the Mercantile across the street. Eddie stood with Merv safely behind the Rolls-Royce Corniche, watching it all unfold. The deafening sound of sirens and spinning red-and-blue lights were a thing to behold. Within a minute or two, there were sixteen people in the street watching the drama. Not what the old girls at the Seniors' were used to. They gathered at their windows up the way, looking on as the police officers took Travis out in handcuffs, then wriggling, screaming, Rhonda.

"Tell 'em it's your fuckin' money, Travis! Tell 'em!"

Merv and Eddie, Darren and Beth, Stephen Coutts, and a dozen or so others gathered in the road, watching as the officers pressed Travis and Rhonda against cruisers. They watched as the police searched their pockets. They watched as officers removed suitcases, rubber tubs, cardboard boxes, and plastic milk crates. All stuffed full with neatly bundled cash. Red-faced with fury and terror, hair falling in her eyes, hands cuffed behind her back, Rhonda wiggled and twisted. She surveyed the onlookers and screamed at them, "Don't fuckin' look at me, you fuckin' assholes. Fuck off!" An officer admonished her to quiet down.

The white evidence van arrived to collect the cash. Uniformed and plain clothes officers mixed and conferred in and out of the Mercantile. Notes and photos were taken. Sirens and lights, eventually turned off. The action died down. Shocked townies slowly dispersed. Merv went back to an oil change, the McIntyres to the pharmacy and liquor outlet, and Stephen Coutts to whatever it was Stephen Coutts did.

After Travis and Rhonda were placed in separate cruisers, Eddie walked haltingly across the road with his pulled hamstring and swollen ankle. A handful of officers watched impassively as Eddie approached the cruiser Travis had been placed in. He looked in to see Travis twitching and gyrating, his face its usual sickly pallor. Eddie spoke to him through the closed window. "Don't say anything. Nothing. Understand?" Eddie asked. Travis nodded. Eddie tapped on the window. "You'll be all right, Trav."

As he turned and began making his way back across the road, Eddie heard Rhonda's muffled calls through the closed window of the other cruiser. He stopped briefly in the middle of the road, turned, and saw her staring at him through the glass.

"Eddie, help! Get me out of here! Help me. Help me, you fucker! Gimme a cigarette!" Eddie stood in the middle of the road, watching Rhonda with her running mascara, smeared lipstick, and messed hair. He wanted to feel sorry for her but couldn't. He couldn't find an ounce of sympathy for the woman who had allowed her own son to be punished for her avarice. A woman whose only interest in her son's freedom from incarceration was her desire for the money he generated. A woman who had rapaciously preyed upon his merciless addiction. Eddie raised his eyebrows and shook his head.

Rhonda pushed her fallen, sixty-eight-year-old face closer to the glass. Tears filled her eyes. Eddie watched as her lips silently formed the words, "Please. I'll suck you off."

The day had finally arrived. Over his many years and decades, Eddie had wondered whether or when this day would ever come. Edward R. Novak had finally found the perp he would not defend. Eddie turned and hobbled the rest of the way across the road back to Merv's. He took a fifty-dollar bill from his pocket and went to the service bay to pay for the gas. Merv barely glanced at him from the underside of the vehicle hoisted on the lift.

"No charge, Eddie."

"I beg your pardon, Mervin?"

"Take your girl for dinner. Tell that young lady, I'd like to meet her one of these days." Eddie glimpsed a tiny smile at the corners of Merv's mouth. It wasn't like Merv to turn away Eddie's money. Merv never offered so much as a free top-up of washer fluid. Eddie respected that. Merv was making a living. Today, however, strange dogs had been loosed. Eddie wondered what was meant by it. He tried to process it as he shuffled back to the Rolls taking up space at Merv's pump. He regarded Merv, working away underneath some local's old beater. He smiled as he pulled out of the station lot onto the road. Merv was a friend of his.

The uproar done, townsfolk continued about their business. Travis and Rhonda were carted away. The Mercantile lights were shut off and the door locked. Eddie quietly rolled out of town. A single police cruiser remained on the roadside at the concession intersection out to Eddie's lake. Eddie stopped at the stop sign. He sat looking. Waiting. His old friend raised his head from the notes he was making behind the wheel. Detachment Commander Stan Kazubowski, a man Eddie had known well near forty years, looked to Eddie and flashed a knowing smile. The men exchanged a simple nod before Eddie rounded the corner and headed home for his final night of the season.

Wind pushed aside the cloud gloom. The clearing let afternoon sun shine through to Eddie's rear-view mirror. He adjusted its angle from his eyes to see the road ahead. The adjusted reflection flooded the Rolls with warm amber light. Eddie crested the hills and took in the expanse of glittering autumn leaves stretched out as far as the horizon. He never tired of this. Eddie reached the drive shed and stowed the Rolls-Royce Corniche.

Slowed by his ankle and hamstring, Eddie plodded slowly and carefully along the trail. There was no threat of darkness just yet, but Eddie wasn't taking any chances. Not with the events he was facing tomorrow. Eddie climbed the granite outcropping just up above the slope down to his cabin. He sat in his spot and looked over the treetops to the azure sky streaked with wisps of yellow and orange above the pink cliffs across the lake. He smoked a cigarette and pondered the day. He considered its rich irony. Rhonda's despicable, usurious grasping had pushed beyond even Eddie Novak's tenuous standard of decency. So far beyond, in fact, he was revulsed by the very idea of assisting her. And then there was the inevitable fact. Even if he'd wanted to help Rhonda, he couldn't. Owing to his own despicable behaviour, Edward R. Novak was no longer licensed to practise law.

Eddie finished his smoke and inched his way down to the cabin. He lit a fire in the wood stove and put the kettle on. Eddie laid back in his recliner and waited for the kettle to boil.

Lounging, Eddie read an old issue of the *New Yorker* from his kindling pile. He sipped his tea and ate a pear. He smoked cigarettes and hummed Rachmaninoff, Piano Concerto no. 3. The hours passed, and it was time for slumber. Eddie stoked the fire before burrowing into his bed. Nights had grown uncomfortably cold, and by morning, with the fire out, Eddie could see his breath on waking. But he was comfortable and warm now. His hamstring and ankle still sore but not unbearable.

Eddie lay awake, pondering the potential outcomes for young Travis. He had little doubt that Travis's desperation for a fix would render him capable of doing or saying whatever he needed to do or say to get back on the street. All of which meant that he would most certainly roll on his mother. She was the fish they were after: the planner, plotter, and profiteer. On the promise of Travis's testimony against his mother, Karen Mulgrave would no doubt accept a guilty plea to summary mischief without pursuit of the other charges. Eddie reckoned by the number of boxes he'd seen, the police had taken several hundred thousand dollars from the Mercantile basement. It galled Eddie that Rhonda had refused Travis money for a lawyer; money Eddie knew she had all along.

Of all the undignified perversities Eddie had involved himself in, a failed sexual escapade with a drug dealer had to be his nadir. Eddie added his entanglement with Rhonda to the mental list of disgraceful conduct no daughter should come to find out about her father. With luck, the remaining discolouration under his eyes would abate before meeting Melanie. Eddie lay awake, trying to calm himself, trying to quell the rising tide of shame and remorse. To be rejected by his own daughter would surely be the end of him. Whatever resolution Eddie believed he had come to about attempting contact with Melanie, he could not fully suppress his pangs of fear and angst.

On top of his angst, Eddie had pressing things to work through. Tomorrow, he'd wake and begin a long journey. He needed to finish up the remaining bits of business to close the cabin, get across the trail, stop at the Blu-Jay Motel, shower, shave, dress in his best suit, drive two hours south to the airport, buy a plane ticket, fly to Casper, and find his daughter.

The cut on Eddie's forehead began to itch. The damage of his life was done. He had nothing left to do but apologize. Not in some legal jargon, or baroque, excuse-making letter, but face to face. He'd humble himself, express his truthful sorrow, and leave Melanie to live the rest of her life untouched by the muck and filth of his.

Sleep came fast and heavy. Eddie drifted off. Another season had come and gone. The night air brought a cold, killing frost. Eddie's fire burned hot till three o'clock in the morning. The cold had woken him by quarter after five. By five thirty, Eddie lay shivering. He pulled himself from his bed and walked the cold floor to his wood stove. For the final time this year, he stoked the fire, laid another log on, and returned to bed. He never fully returned to sleep, rolling and tossing in half sleep another hour or so. It was still dark when Eddie sat up to meet what would be a busy day. The swelling in his ankle had subsided but was still sore to stand on. His hamstring still tender when he extended his leg to walk. He'd adopted a shorter gait with a lean to one side to compensate for these injuries.

Teeth brushed, clothing on, Eddie set about his business before the sun rose. He supposed it might be a five- or possibly six-hour trip from Toronto to Casper. If he caught an early afternoon flight, with the time difference, Eddie would get to Wyoming just before dinner. He lit a small new jar candle for better light and a bit more heat. The scent of lavender and vanilla filled the cabin. Eddie generally hated scented candles. This particular one he'd been given by Beth after it failed to sell during the pharmacy's annual fall clearance event. He was unexpectedly comforted and pleased by the aroma.

The wood stove was stoked again. Eddie boiled his remaining two eggs in a pot of water. He sat by the stove and peeled their shells. A tiny dollop of yolk dripped down his chin as he bit into the second egg. The taste struck him as uncommonly delicious.

Shells tossed out the door, Eddie carried on, folding up his blankets, stripping his sheets and pillowcases, gathering his things from the screened-in porch, and bringing them inside.

Eddie gave way to the pressure in his abdomen. He donned his tattered old loafers, his suit coat, and stepped outside to relieve himself. He toddled over to the edge of the forest by the sandy shore, retrieved a cigarette, and smoked while he waited. It was a cool morning but not unseasonal. Lovely in its own way. The minutes passed, and finally his bladder dribbled to a quarter tank.

Eddie watched steam rise from the lake. He couldn't quite identify the curious sensation filling him as the sun came up over the cliffs and trees. A warm front might have been rolling in. Across the water, the rustle of animals bustling through scrub trees sounded behind the driftwood bay. Moose more than likely. Possibly bear on a late-season forage. Eddie welcomed such encounters and visitations. He watched closely, waiting to glimpse the early morning passerby. A quiet thrum began somewhere in the distance. Moose in rut, he surmised.

A visit to the outhouse wouldn't wait. Eddie struggled up the gentle slope behind the cabin for his morning sit-down. He wasn't recovering from his aches as quickly as he might have not so long ago. The rutting call had put Eddie to thinking of a sultry cornet. Tapping his toe, Eddie hummed "Davenport Blues" as best he could recollect its chords. Eddie finished his business greatly unburdened and began the double-check of the cabin and property. He gathered the last of his items and prepared for final departure. It was early still. Eddie was pleased he hadn't overslept and left himself in a rush.

The sun was well up over the cliffs just now, leaving only traces of steam quickly burning off the lake. A bit of sun on his still bruised and cut face would be nice. Eddie teetered down to the sandy shore to take in the warmth. The sun shone, lake glittered, trees sparkled. Sunshine lit Eddie's chest and face gloriously afire. He'd gone to sleep stone-cold sober and woken clear-headed two days in a row. Some magic had come. Eddie looked at the cliffs, the lake, the stunning colour of autumn leaves. He loved all of it. This place was, in its way, Eddie's magnetic north. His compass home.

Way off to the distant south was an intermittent hum. He had much travelling to do and obligations to resolve. But he'd bathe in this moment just as long as he could. Eddie turned his thoughts to the air around him. He couldn't see his breath. No steam remained above the water. The sun felt warm on his face. His chest and body, temperate. Eddie lowered his suit jacket from his shoulders and left it on the grass beside him. He pulled his ancient collared shirt over his head and left it atop his suit jacket. A soft breeze tousled the grey hair on Eddie's chest as he slipped out of his shoes and socks, pants and underwear. The hum in the distance drew closer.

Eddie waded into the freezing water. He staggered out to his waist before plunging under. The bracing water caught his breath, slowed his limbs, and tore at his temples. He pushed forward, swimming under the surface as far as his legs and arms would take him. He lifted his head from the water, gasping. His teeth chattered, and his jaw shook. Still, he gathered himself, refusing to concede. Eddie treaded water a moment. It came to him just then as he scanned the driftwood bay and the cliffs across the lake. Schubert, Quartet no. 14, in D Minor. *Death and the Maiden*.

Eddie's frigid reverie abruptly ended to a loud revving noise. He turned his body to the shore where the sound was coming from. The rumbling startled him. It couldn't be much past nine in the morning. Eddie pushed his shaking body toward land, his eyes scanning for the source of the sound. Then through the trees high up on the granite outcropping, a vehicle appeared. An all-terrain four-wheeler darted across the trail, passing quickly back into the bush in the direction of the drive shed and road. Eddie thought he'd seen an older man in a green jumpsuit driving the ATV.

Eddie swam as fast as his freezing cold body would take him, the frigid water prickling his skin numb. His last ounce of energy escaped him as his feet finally touched bottom. He stood uneasily. He steadied himself, then walked in halting steps, his body shaking, his head reeling. Floating stars filled his eyes as he trudged up the cold lake bed. Up ahead past the cabin, his eyes caught movement where the trail met the clearing. A figure emerged into the open space. Eddie lurched forward, squinting to see. The movement stopped. Eddie could see the silhouette of a person. It moved again, descending the hill toward the cabin. Eddie stood knee deep in the freezing water. The figure drew closer. He shook his head and blinked to clear his eyes. A woman appeared there, no more than ten metres from him now.

His breath shallow, ribs, leg, and ankle throbbing, Eddie inched himself from the depths in tilting steps. The woman advanced slowly, curiously. She watched as Eddie stepped cold and shaking from water onto dry earth. The two regarded one another in silence. She studied his face, torso, arms, legs, and feet, the yellowing circles beneath his eyes, angry cut across his forehead. Eddie met her eyes and the contours of her familiar features. She smiled and stepped closer. Lurching forward, Eddie staggered close enough to see the exquisite details of her face. He stood before her, naked, battered, faltering. A lump formed in his throat. His shoulders lowered, and his eyes filled. A calm settled in him. She extended her hand and spoke as he took her hand in his.

"Hello, Eddie."

"Hello, Melanie."

Manufactured by Amazon.ca
Bolton, ON